GRANDAD SHINE

Ewan Grant McNeil

Simpson's Memory Box Appeal

The proceeds from sale of this book will be donated
directly to SiMBA

www.simbacharity.org.uk

ABOUT THE AUTHOR

Ewan Grant McNeil was born in Nairn, in the Scottish Highlands in 1969. Coming from a family with a historic passion for storytelling and growing up in a freedom and character-filled council housing estate in the 70s and 80s in that small, Northern Scottish town, he naturally gained a wealth of characters and experiences from which to draw his own stories.

Formerly a freelance cartoonist, medical technician, TEFL teacher, laboratory technician, woodsman, student, oil industry worker, local government worker etc, Ewan recently decided to get his stories from his head and onto paper at last.

This decision to finally do this was not in part inspired by the fact of his sister buying the former house of an unsung, Scottish Victorian author and preacher, George Macdonald, who Ewan had not heard of before. Familiar and respected to this day in the USA, Mr Macdonald is sadly virtually forgotten in his native Scotland – despite him being the mentor to Lewis Carroll and quoted literary inspiration to both C.S Lewis and J.R.R Tolkein.

This book is written at a 'classic' pace and with a central moral message throughout, rather than at the racier, more commercially focused modern pace and style.

It is hoped that readers will gain enjoyment and perhaps something more from reading the book – particularly those affected by the loss of loved ones or who recognize the only real, but basic and deep values in life.

Thanks are offered to those Nairn characters and their loved ones who are characterized in the book who made a positive impression in the author's childhood. Apologies are offered to older readers for the 'artistic licence' of locations in the book around Nairn often having a different role to those they may have had during the WWII era. This was done purposefully, so that younger readers could relate to the locations, given their more recent roles.

COPYRIGHT DETAIL

DEDICATED TO

Shannonka – my eternal star. Never, ever stop believing or let anyone take belief from you. Only the most wonderful, magical and seemingly unbelievable of things are true and eternal, as is the very essence of this story. Without question and unconditionally I eternally love you, I'm proud of you and you're a good girl, no matter what

Zawsze z toba XXX Tato

Adriana, simply and truly my Soul-Mate. More than words

Kocham cie Kochanie XXX

To Grandad McNeil, beloved Starcarer

And 'last', but certainly not least, to my Mother, Evelyn, Daughter of that Star-Carer. Thank you for being my Mother and for teaching me the essence of what is true and eternal by your living example and love – possibly without even knowing it!
The Stars await us all, when it's time – It's going to be one, Great party!

Eternally yours Mum XXX

GRANDAD SHINES STARS

By
Ewan G McNeil

CHAPTER 1 – Wondering

Shannon peeled back the black paper from her bedroom window and stared out through the glass at the twinkling night sky above her. She'd looked up at the moon and stars so many times before. But tonight she wasn't just looking at how beautiful they were, but thinking about just what they could be and thinking how they would look, up close. She wondered *'Is Grandad really up there right now?'* After all, that's where he told her he went at night. He always told her the most wonderful stories and they all seemed so real. Her favourites were when he'd tell her how he'd fly up into the twinkling night sky on his bicycle to shine those stars up there. And he'd tell her how after he'd finished shining those stars about how he'd park his bike by a little cottage on the dusty moon and stop for a chat and a cup of tea with a man who lived there. And he'd told her all about this again today. Shannon had just started doing a project at school all about stars and planets with her teacher, but there was no mention of Grandad at all, or at least not yet. Up until now she'd just thought that Grandad's stories, especially of him shining the stars were all true. But now that she was eight years old she began to wonder to herself just what was true and what was just make-believe. Maybe he just told her these stories to cheer her up and make magical things seem real. She scrunched up her eyes to see as well as she could and pressed her nose right up against the cold, wet window to get the best possible chance of seeing Grandad up there on his bike, her hair glowing in the moonlight. After a while she turned to her doll on the bed next to her and asked *'Do you think Grandad's really up there Mrs Beasley?'* Of course, Shannon got no reply and turned back to stare up at the twinkling sky again.

She stayed there for a long time, until she grew tired and decided that the moon and stars were just *too* far away to see Grandad, even if he was up there. She got into her bed, but left the curtains open so that she could keep an eye on the moon through that gap in the black paper, just in case she saw Grandad flying about up there on his bike!

She looked up at the sheet of black paper she'd peeled off, lying there on the windowsill above her bed. She knew that she should really put it back on the window to cover it up again. Everyone had to. Apparently it was in case some nasty enemy aeroplanes flew over, saw their house lights shining down on the ground below and decided to drop some bombs on them. It all sounded impossible and daft to her! This is Nairn! A small town in the North of Scotland. Why on earth would someone want to drop bombs up here? This 'war' was so annoying to her. She could hardly remember what it was like to see the bright streetlamps on, it seemed so long ago. And she could only dream of what it must be like to have a whole bar of chocolate to herself again, because now there was so little of it about. She knew very well that she might get in trouble for not putting the black paper back up on the window, but all she wanted to do right now was look up at the moon through the window and imagine Grandad and his friend in a cottage up there, telling each other stories over a cup of tea. Could it possibly be true?

As she started to drift off into sleep, a bittersweet thought suddenly came to her mind. 'Could Daddy be looking up at the same moon as I am right now?' She missed him so much. All she knew was that he had to go away with the army to fight in France. Far above being annoyed about the darkness in the streets and the lack of chocolate, missing her Daddy was what she hated most of all about this war. She felt a tear drop from her eye and start to roll down her face onto her pillow as she thought about him. She smiled and blew a kiss to the moon, *just* in case he would somehow feel it. She said her prayers and her usual special one for her Daddy and for all other people caught up in this nasty war. As she did every night now, she closed her eyes and imagined him being next to her and saying to her what he told her every night before her bedtime story: "*I love you, I'm proud of you and you're a good girl!*" She slowly fell asleep, the moonlight warmly shining on her blankets.

That night she dreamt about Grandad shining stars and woke up excited about it all the next morning, wondering whether it could all be true. She went downstairs to the kitchen to see Mum. Over a toast and marmalade breakfast she thought she'd try to find out. "Mum, Grandad was telling me again that at night he goes up to the stars and the moon to dust and shine them!"

Mum smiled at the comment warmly "Really? I've not heard him mention that in a long, long time. Well, they're nice stories Shannon" Mum's face changed and she said carefully " but I'm sorry to say, they're just not true. I suppose that he told you that he goes up to the stars on his rickety old bike? And that the bike's magic?" she smiled.

"Well....yes!" Shannon murmured

"So, when you go on the bar of his bike, does it seem 'magic' to you?" Mum joked.

Shannon was disappointed and lowered her eyes to look at the floor, feeling silly "Well, I *suppose* not Mum."

Shannon's Mum noticed her disappointment and said

"Shannon – do you remember that time when you were a toddler and you saw that ship on fire?"

Shannon remembered it well. In fact, it was her first ever memory and she could still see it in her head so clearly. A neighbour had knocked on their house door late that night, waking everyone in the house up. She remembered Grandad taking her out the front door and lifting her up high on his shoulders and walking over to where lots of the neighbours were standing on their hill, looking down towards the sea. Their faces were lit up by a distant fire. A ship was in flames on the sea. Shannon remembered how sad Grandad was to see it. Mum continued "Well Shannon, that was a terrible night and a terrible thing that happened to that boat. You might not remember it all, but I remember Grandad noticed you looking upset and he asked you to look up at the stars above you, instead of at the burning ship. He wanted you to see something magical, instead of something so sad. That's the first time that I heard him whispering that story about cleaning the stars to you, pointing up at the sky. He loves you and wants you to believe in magical things. That's no bad thing Shannon. But a story's just…well, a story!"

As Mum finished talking she felt bad, seeing that Shannon looked so sad about finding this out. She knelt down in front of her and lifted her chin gently to face her "Look Shannon. When I was a little girl your Grandad told me the same things. We were doing a project on stars and planets in class, just like you are now. I remember how *wonderful* and sparkly the night sky looked after he'd told me that he cleaned them and it filled me with *wonderful* thoughts. I wrote about it in my schoolbook as part of my class project. My teacher read it out in class and I felt so bad when everyone laughed. I felt very silly. I asked your Grandad about it when I got home. He saw that I'd been crying and asked me why. So I told him. I could see in his eyes as I told him that he felt terrible. Granny even shouted at him for telling me stories and she told me that it all wasn't true! So *please*, *don't* make the same mistake Shannon."

Shannon was close to tears "But *why* would Grandad *lie* Mum?"
Mum put her hand on Shannon's head and crouched down, smiling at her. "He's not really 'lying' Shannon. He loves you *so* much and just wants you to believe in *magical* things. That's not *wrong*, surely? Oh Shannon, I'll tell you what. If you want to believe what Grandad told you then you go ahead and believe it. Goodness knows, it might even be true after all!" she smiled as she shrugged her shoulders. "But if you *do want to believe him, please* keep it to yourself, all right?" she winked.
Shannon wasn't really happy with this, as it was such an exciting story, but she agreed not to tell anyone. But deep inside, she still hoped it could still possibly be true. "All right Mum." she sighed.

That night when Mum walked Shannon up the stairs to bed she noticed that she was still a bit sad. She read her a bedtime story and said her prayers with her, including those special ones for Daddy and kissed her "Goodnight, God-bless" before going downstairs again. Shannon thought about their talk as she peeled back that piece of black paper and stared up at the moon again. She lay in her bed holding her dolly to her tummy. She felt empty, like something wonderful had been stolen out of her. She turned her dolly to face her and said "It was a nice story wasn't it, Mrs Beasley? But I'm sorry to say that Mum said that it wasn't true about Grandad shining the stars." She felt like crying when she looked into her doll's face, imagining that even her dolly looked disappointed and felt bad that she'd told *her*! She turned to face the moon's glow again and stared up at it. But suddenly it didn't seem so special at all. Now the night sky just looked like a big, dark blanket, cold and empty, except for a big yellow circle and a few tiny, faraway lights. *How* could she believe that it was anything else, so far away? In fact, if anything, it almost seemed like an *annoying* thing now. After all, when it shone really brightly, it only made the houses down here easier for bomber planes to see! Then she thought about Mum getting teased by the other girls for believing Grandad's stories and how sad Grandad must have been to know that his story ended up making Mum cry. She *hated* to think of Mum or Grandad sad, but was also so upset about what Mum said about the stars themselves. She *so* wanted to believe in them, only now they were just 'things'. But as she lay there a *sudden, hopeful* thought came to her. She quickly sat up and turned to the moon, then back to her dolly and wiped the tears from her face with her pyjama sleeve. 'But wait a minute!' she whispered excitedly to herself '*maybe* Grandad just told Mum that it wasn't true because he didn't want the girls to laugh at her about it at school. Maybe it *is* true Mrs Beasley. Yes, that *must* be it! " She went to sleep feeling much better again. And facing the stars and moon through the window, they suddenly seemed to twinkle brightly again, maybe even stronger than ever before! She drifted off to sleep, smiling again.

The next morning as Shannon sat in Mrs Grant's class getting told more about the wonderful stars, comets, meteors and lots of other things in space with funny names, she couldn't help but secretly think of Grandad being up there. The class painted planet shapes and a big sun and stuck them onto a huge sheet of black paper. Then they cut out star shapes from silver foil. As Shannon was cutting one out she held it up to the light, turned it slightly and stared as the glow from the class lights reflected on it, shining brightly onto her face. She imaged her Grandad shining it high up in the sky and thought how wonderful it must be to do that.

Shannon's best pal Louisa saw her staring at the paper and wondered what she was doing. "Emmm...are you *all right* Shannon?"

Shannon suddenly stopped her daydream and smiled at her pal. "Yes, fine." she said, as she put the shape on the desk. She smiled to herself and thought 'I'll bet Grandad's stars shine brighter than these!'

After school, Shannon always went round to Grandad's house, because Mum worked in a bakers shop in town. She loved going round to Grandad's. Granny was great at baking and made the most fantastic cakes and buns. Even *better* than the ones Mum made at work! Grandad was always great fun and so full of things to say and stories to tell. Shannon used to listen to the Roy West Cowboy Show on the radio with him; and he was great at cowboy impressions. But today Shannon wasn't just walking to their house – she was running! She had so many questions to ask Grandad. She ran past a convoy line of army traffic - trundling tanks, jeeps, lorries and even some donkeys on their way to wherever they were going. She was used to seeing these, so they no longer appeared to be special at all. She raced past Grandad's painting workshop at the top of the railway station hill and soon she arrived, puffing at his house - Maybank.

It seemed huge to Shannon. Big and made of sandy stone like a mini-castle and with a huge garden round the back. She called the garden '*The Prairie*', which Mum though was '*nice*'. Maybe the garden didn't seem so *big* to a grown up! Shannon pulled open the gate, raced to the door, turned the big metal handle and stepped inside. She slung her schoolbag onto the floor and got annoyed that her coat got stuck for a while on her arm as she raced to get it off, until she eventually yanked it off and threw it over the coat-peg.

"Hi Grandad!" she shouted as she puffed into the living room.

Grandad's pipe smoke rose like a sea fog around his wiggly ears. His domed head was edged by white hair at the sides and he was dressed in his usual white, ironed shirt and turn-up tweed trousers. His face was permanently wrinkled, especially around his gleaming eyes, caused by long years of cheeky smiling. He looked up at her through his, round, bottle-thick glasses over the sports pages of the newspaper where he sat. "My! You're looking out of breath and full of life Shannon. What's the hurry today then?"

"Oh, nothing really Grandad." There was a short silence as she looked around the room, sat down and twiddled her thumbs. Grandad beamed a knowing smile as he pretended to read the newspaper again, knowing that a question was coming from her any second. It soon came.

"Grandad..."

He lowered the newspaper again with a quick rustle and smiled across at her. "Yes Shannon?"

"Well, I was just sort of wondering....."

He lowered the pages further to his lap

"Yeeeess?" he joked.

"Well, you know that you tell me that you sometimes go up to shine the stars at night?" She felt guilty about asking him the next question, but bleated it out. "Well - is it true Grandad?"

He nodded his head as if he'd been asked that before and was expecting it. He sat forward, folded his newspaper, slowly removed his glasses and put them on the small table next to him, by the fire. He smiled at her and said.

"Well, what do *you* think?"

"Emmmmm." she paused

He put his finger to her mouth to stop her; and let her take her time to answer. "I'll tell you what" whispered Grandad" How about a nice sweety first? But don't tell Granny or she'll nag at me for spoiling your tea!" he winked.

She raised her eyebrows and whispered back "Sounds good to me Grandad!"

He held open a bag of Fairy Mints and she plopped one into her mouth. "Well Shannon, all I can say to you is that if you think for yourself and believe deep inside yourself that something's true, then it *is* true. And *nobody* can argue with that!"

This just confused Shannon. "Yes Grandad, but can you not just tell me if you shine the stars or not?"

Grandad smiled "Well Shannon, what's more important is not to ask me that, but to ask yourself if you *believe something so magical can be* true."

Shannon still didn't know what to think, but didn't want to upset Grandad by asking him again.

Suddenly she heard Granny calling from the kitchen.

"Shannon. Do you want to help me make some iced biscuits again tonight, my dear?"

No other baking in the world compared to Granny's and her iced jammy biscuits were amazing.

"Coming!" She *raced* through to the kitchen. Granny was a lovely little lady, quite round with grey hair, shiny skin and smelt of lavender. She almost always wore a lovely flowery *'pinnie'* (apron) in the house, except on Sundays, when she went to church and wore her wonderful hats and sparkling brooches. Shannon found her kneading some cake mix on the work surface, which sent up a small cloud of flour around her. She walked across the room and gave Granny a 'hello' kiss.

"Was school good today?" asked Granny.

"Yes"

"What did you learn?"

"'Can't remember!"

Granny raised her eyebrows nodded to herself, smiling "Aye, well. Some things never change!" They talked and baked together, but as Granny turned to put the oven on, Shannon decided to ask *her* about Grandad shining the stars; and if it was all true. She stopped and looked at Shannon, nodded her head and wiped some flour from her nose with her wrist. "Well Shannon, what do you think yourself?" Shannon gasped. This annoyed Shannon a bit.

"Aww Granny, that's what *Grandad* said - and I *still* don't know!"

"All right Shannon, put it like this. Do you think that Julius Caesar was a real person?"

"Of *course* he was, Granny! We got a project about him at school."

"But you've never seen him Shannon. The *only* reason that you think that he was real is because some people *told* you that he was. It's very probable that he *did* exist and was an amazing person. But although I may look about 2,000 years old to you, I never met the man myself! So *if you can believe other people who tell you about Julius Caesar, why do you find it* hard to believe Grandad when he tells you that he shines the stars?" she smiled. Granny saw that Shannon probably looked even more confused than before and said "Shannon, I'll tell you what. If I was a wee girl again like you are, I'd personally choose to believe the magical stories that Grandad tells you for as long as you like. But I'll tell you something very important too, Shannon. If your heart tells you to believe in magical stories, please don't tell anyone else about them, or you may end up getting hurt. Do you promise?"

Shannon nodded and remembered that Mum had told her the same thing. She could see that Granny was very serious as she spoke. But she was also happy that both Granny and Grandad didn't say for sure that the stories were just made up, as she thought they would. Shannon certainly still hoped that they were true and quite soon she would find out for sure in the most amazing way.

CHAPTER 2 – Looking

Ding-a-ling-a-ling-a-ling-a-ling! The playtime bell echoed around the school as Shannon and all of her classmates cleared their desks and scrambled out into the playground. She was *so* excited to think that Grandad's star-shining stories could still be true and was *bursting* to tell someone, but remembered Mum and Granny's warnings about what can happen if you do! She joined Louisa on an empty spot on the grass and sat down. Shannon just *had* to tell her best pal secretly about Grandad's stories or she'd *explode*! She'd sneaked out a couple of bottles of homemade 'sugarelly' liquorice juice from home that she'd made up and gave a bottle to Louisa, who was absolutely delighted to get it. Louisa was madly shaking her bottle up, her thumb over the top, when Shannon spoke.

"Louisa, can I tell you a secret?"

"Of course!" she said, taking her thumb off the top of the bottle and letting some of the tasty froth ooze out.

"And you promise that you'll keep this secret to yourself?"

"Don't ask daft questions, I'm your *friend* amn't I?" she said, before gulping down a mouthful of the sweet- liquorice drink and wiping her mouth on her sleeve.

Shannon went on to tell Louisa all about Grandad's star-shining stories and that she believed that maybe the stories could be true. Now *all* children at that time liked sugarelly and Louisa absolutely *loved* it! But even *she* stopped gulping it down, amazed at what Shannon was saying and she seemed to believe what she was hearing. She was her friend, after all. This made Shannon all the more excited, but it also made her speak more and more *loudly* as she told Louisa more. But as her voice got louder and more excited she was suddenly interrupted by a loud, nasty laugh from behind her. Shannon suddenly stopped and looked up to see the horrible bully, Veronica Cumberland from two classes up looking down at her - and realised that she must have heard *everything*! Veronica was a *nasty* girl in so many ways. And there was *nothing* she liked more than picking on younger girls and calling them names. Her long, pointed face sneered at Shannon through her narrow, thick-rimmed glasses.

"So your silly old Grandad shines the stars then, does he? Do you really believe that? I suppose he paints them as well, with smelly old paint from his workshop?" She shouted to her friend and fellow-bully, Marjory, who was leaning against the school wall. "Do you hear this Marjory? Apparently Shannon's Grandad shines stars in the sky at night!"

Marjory started cackling like an old witch and came over. Shannon groaned and blushed with what was coming. Those two *horrible* girls laughed and sneered at Shannon, pretending that they were shining imaginary stars above their heads, sniggering nastily all the time.

"How can he manage that then, when his old legs can hardly walk?" they laughed. "Does he fly up there on a walking stick then? Maybe he uses his rickety old bike to fly on!"

Shannon knew that was exactly how Grandad said he flew up to the stars, but that it was just a lucky and *nasty* guess Veronica had made. Shannon decided that she'd had enough and cried out: "You leave my Grandad alone!"

"Ooooooooohhhhhhhh" the girls pretended to be scared. "What are you going to do about it Shannon? B*ite* me with his false teeth?" sneered Marjory.

"Stop it!" shouted Louisa "Shannon's my friend, leave her alone!"

"Oh, You've got someone else who believes that rubbish - and *so tough*, too!" Veronica pushed little Louisa's shoulder, just to show who was the biggest. The wicked girls just laughed even louder as they walked away. "Come on Marjory, we've got some *planet* brushing to do! See you later Shannon!" Their laughs slowly disappeared. Louisa reached across to Shannon, who was now in floods of tears and hugged her.

"It's okay Shannon. Do you want to tell the teacher on them?"

"No thanks" Shannon replied "Telling someone about this has made me lots of problems already! I should have listened to my Mum and Granny and kept my big mouth shut!"

That afternoon in class Shannon was very quiet. All she wanted to do was to go home and cry. At home-time Louisa walked with her to the school front-gate as usual. She had her arm around Shannon, who was still upset about what happened at lunchtime. As they chatted and started to cheer up, they suddenly heard a familiar, *screeching* voice and laughter behind them.

 "Anyone got a duster on them? I've got some *star*-cleaning to do tonight!" Veronica cackled.

"Oh no! Not *her*!" said Louisa.

Shannon ran down the pavement away from the school gates leaving Veronica's laughter behind her, her throat getting sorer by the second. Sure enough, Shannon's tears began to flow as she ran. She only stopped to wipe the tears from her face just before opening the gate at Grandad's house.

She quietly opened the door and slung her bag and coat down on the floor. Today was the day she'd usually listen to The Roy West Wild West Radio Show with Grandad. But instead of rushing in for the show, she raced into the bathroom and closed the door shut. She looked in the mirror to check her face and *immediately* burst into tears. She put her arms on the sink to rest her crying face and put the tap on fast to stop Grandad or Granny hearing her cry. Soon she heard a gentle tap on the bathroom door.

"Shannon... Are you okay in there?" came Grandad's voice from the hallway.

Shannon tried her best to put on a normal voice.

"Yes Grandad, I'm fine. I'll be out in a wee while."

She tried to wash away the tears and redness from her eyes as best as she could and after a few minutes she opened the door of the bathroom and looked out. The hall was empty. She noticed that Grandad had picked up her coat and schoolbag and hung them up neatly on the coat-hook and knew that he'd be through in the sitting room. She walked in and saw him peering over the newspaper at her. He spoke softly and slowly.

"Hi Shannon"

"Hi Grandad"

"How was school today then?" he said as he folded his newspaper and sat up.

Shannon looked down, trying to disguise the redness around her eyes. She found that she couldn't reply. Instead she found a cry coming out of her throat and she rushed towards him in his chair. He hugged her, not saying a word and just patted her back. He was always good at not asking too much until it was time to talk. She fell asleep in his arms and he lay her down on the sofa to sleep out the sadness.

She woke up later and saw Grandad sitting in his armchair by the fire, reading the horseracing pages of his newspaper. He looked over and whispered

"Hello Sleepy-eyes, would you like to have some tea now?"

"I'm not really hungry, Grandad."

"Come on, once you get something down you, you'll feel *much* better." Grandad winked, as he got up and went to the dining table by the window. He started to lay the table, but Shannon soon got up and helped him. Grandad turned to her "You *do* know that you've slept through The Roy West Cowboy Show on the radio, don't you?"

"That's okay Grandad" replied Shannon "I don't really *want* to hear it today."

Grandad stood up and put his hands on his sides and pretended to be amazed in his 'cowboy voice' "*What*? *You* miss The Roy West Show? It's not like our little Cowgirl to do that, now is it?" he joked, before sticking his thumb up and back in front of his forehead, like he was tipping an imaginary cowboy hat. Shannon couldn't help but smile. There was no mention of Shannon's teary face at teatime from anyone, although Granny gave Shannon an extra helping of iced biscuits at the end of tea, to cheer her up. Granny later asked Shannon why she was crying earlier, but didn't look at all happy when she heard the reason for Shannon's tears!

Tonight was a night that Shannon stayed over at Granny's house. Later that night she lay in her bed reading a comic annual. After the teasing at school today she didn't feel like peeking out of the window at the stars. But soon her reading became disturbed by hearing Granny and Grandad talking downstairs. It sounded like Granny was telling Grandad off and was angry with him. Shannon tossed back her covers and crept quietly out onto the landing, listening to what was being said below.

"Oh, you know *well* why Shannon's been crying, don't you?" scolded Granny

"It's *you* telling her about going up to the stars. Just like you did with her Mother years ago. Our poor Evelyn was teased at school for that too. *Why* don't you just keep quiet about it all, eh Jimmy? *Why* mention it? Or at least why not remind her to keep such stories to herself, before she makes a fool of herself by telling folk?"

Shannon couldn't really hear what Grandad said back. Her breathing disturbed what she could hear and she tried to hold her breath to hear more. All she could hear were sounds from Grandad agreeing with Granny. He sounded so sorry and sad.

Shannon didn't like to hear them arguing and hadn't really heard them argue like this before. What's more, she *certainly* didn't want to hear that it was all just a *story again*! She slowly edged her way back to her bed, clicked off the lamp, took down the black paper from the window and peered out again at the stars. She heard herself saying up to them "That's it! You're just far away balls of fire, aren't you?" before reaching up and blocking them from view again with the black paper. She hugged her pillow as she slowly drifted towards sleep. It had been a long day. She thought of that *horrible* Veronica. As she began to drift off, she heard Grandad gently closing the front door behind him as he went out, as he often did. But then a wakening thought came to her. Granny never actually said that Grandad *never* cleaned the stars at night. She only said that he shouldn't have *said* anything! This thought annoyed Shannon, as it was keeping her awake now. She *still* didn't know if it was true or not. '*Right*!' She thought to herself. 'I'm going to find out *once and for all*! I'm *going* to see where Grandad goes at night. Right *now*!'

She threw back her blankets, got out of bed, switched on the lamp and quietly rushed her clothes on. She looked around the room, then back down at her pillow. She took it, a spare blanket from the wardrobe and a couple of toys and shaped them into a pile in the middle of her bed. She folded the blanket back over it all and patted it into a shape that might have looked a bit like her sleeping, *just* in case Granny looked in her room when she was out. She quietly opened the door and crept as quietly as she possibly could along the landing, *hardly* breathing. She slowly placed down the stairs, one by one, trying to avoid any creaks. Granny often knitted quietly late at night, but tonight she was listening to a radio drama, which was a bit noisy. This made it easier for Shannon not to be heard. She got to the open living room door and looked through the crack behind it. Granny wasn't there, so she must be in the kitchen. Shannon took the chance and then quickly crept past towards the front door, slipped on her shoes and coat and slowly turned the doorknob as the cool night air breezed in. Out she stepped into the night and managed to get the door closed behind her without a sound. She turned round and tiptoed along the edge of the cool grass, in case the gravel on the path was too noisy. She looked back at the front windows of the house and felt guilty that she'd sneaked out. But she just *had* to follow Grandad and find out if what he said about going to the stars was true, once and *for all*! She slowly closed the gate. *Now* she felt she'd *done* it, got out without being discovered! The field across the road shone light blue with moonlight and the sky was so full of glinting stars. She pulled her coat up tight to her neck to keep the cold night air out. She walked down the colourless road, past menacing shadows of hedges and walls that looked so much like waiting monsters at that time of night. She jogged past them and down the road. "*Right!*" she said to herself "*Where's* Grandad?"

As she turned the corner at the bottom of the road, she looked far into the distance, and saw the dark figure of a man. Could it be *him*? She raced on along the pavement, keeping hidden and close to the hedges. Soon she saw that special walk and cap of the figure ahead. It was *definitely* Grandad! She stayed her distance and carefully followed him down town, past the school, their family church and the police station. She watched from behind a bush as he crossed the road, took off his cap and walked through the front door of the Community Centre. Shannon and her pals just called it the 'Centre'.

Her heart sank. "Is that *it*?" she thought "He's *only* going to the 'Centr, probably just to play cards with his old friends. *That's hardly* cleaning stars!" She felt like crying and sat on a wall for a few minutes. That it was it for definite then - Grandad's stories must have all been just make-believe and it looked like Mum was right after all. She thought of Veronica, laughing at her for believing such stories. Of course, Veronica wasn't a nice girl, in fact she was quite *horrible* at the best of times, but looking up to the cold night sky above her Shannon suddenly felt *so* stupid.

She crossed the empty road to the 'Centre to peek in and see if she could see Grandad anyway. She still loved him more than the whole, wide world and it would be nice to see him enjoying himself with his friends. She stood on a large rock and peeped through a small gap in a darkened side-window into the games room, where cards were played. She could just make out what was happening through a small gap in the black curtains. Sure enough, there was Grandad and a few of his old friends, including Granny's brother, Uncle Tuppence. They were dealing out cards and smiling away, with cups of tea and biscuits on the low tables. Behind Grandad was an old, broken radio that Shannon had seen on youth nights at the 'Centre. It was a large wooden one, with the strange sounding words 'Ad astra' carved on it in fancy writing. Shannon and her pals used to laugh at it, because it looked so old and useless to them. She kept on watching Grandad playing cards and laughing with his friends, which made her smile, too.

After Shannon had waited for a chilly hour or so, all of the men in the room had gone, except for Grandad, Uncle Tuppence and another man in dark glasses and a hat, who hadn't been playing cards, but had just sat down laughing with the rest. He had his back towards Shannon and she couldn't figure out who he could be. They started to pack up the cards as Grandad stood up, looked out of the far door into the corridor to check on something, before locking the door behind him. He went over to the old radio. This was puzzling to Shannon. What was he doing? His two friends sat themselves down in front of the radio as Grandad tapped the side of it and a little light came on inside it. "Oh - I never knew that old thing worked!" Shannon thought. But what she saw next didn't just surprise her, it absolutely amazed her!

Chapter 3 - Discovering

Grandad grabbed the lid of the radio and somehow *flipped* it over, to
show a big, shiny semi-circle now sticking out of the top of it, like a black
glass dome. Uncle Tuppence and the other man just sat relaxed in their
chairs like they'd seen it all before. Grandad took a little tin pot very
carefully from his pocket and dipped his finger in. It seemed to twinkle
brightly with *whatever* was in that pot. He rubbed his sparkling finger
gently over the top of the black dome and *then* Shannon saw it! Suddenly
the dome started to *glow* with the most *beautiful* blues, greens and whites
she had ever seen. Such an old, battered radio, with such a *wonderful*
bright and colourful picture surprise hidden inside! As she looked more
she soon realised *what* it was. It was a beautiful picture of the earth, *just*
as it looked in her school geography books. *So* many questions flooded
through her head. *Who* would have made this? Why was it hidden inside
an old *radio*? What made it *glow* so beautifully? She'd never *seen* such a
beautiful glow like it before. What kind of lightbulb was in there? Was the
picture *moving*? Swirling? Was she *imagining* things? She kept staring at
it through that gap between the curtains, as Grandad and his friends got
together some mugs for tea, not really paying much attention to the
pictures on the dome. She was amazed, but knew she had to get back
before Granny discovered she wasn't in bed. But as she turned to go her
head whipped back to the window, her eyes open wide. Did she *really*
see that? Grandad's hand moved over the top of the dome, close, but not
touching it. But as he gently lowered his hand close to the dome, the
whole 'picture' moved *with* it, like Grandad was shifting his view of the
dome by magic! He then gently placed his hand on the top, before pulling
it slowly up above his head, as he grinned in delight. A golden light *shone*

like a long piece of glowing elastic between his hand and the dome. The 'picture' slowly grew darker, until it was almost black again. But soon within that blackness appeared twinkling dots. Shannon gasped as she realised...they were *stars*! The dome was showing the night sky. Grandad lowered his hand away from the dome and rested it by his side, then looked down, deeply into it. As he did, Shannon noticed a few white lines racing across the dome.

"It's moving - they're...they're *shooting* stars!" she gasped to herself. *This really was* something *special*.

She stared, wide-eyed as Grandad next took an artists' paintbrush and pointed at various stars on the dome, talking as Uncle Tuppence scribbled notes on some paper and the other man with the hat and glasses listened and nodded. After a few minutes, she watched Grandad flip the radio lid back over, hiding the dome again. Uncle Tuppence ripped the pages he'd written on out of the notebook and handed them to Grandad. The man with the hat and dark glasses shook Grandad and Tuppence's hands and walked over to the piano in the far corner and sat down in front of it, as Grandad and Tuppence went to the door to leave the room. Shannon ducked down below the window again as they stood, in case they saw her. She could just hear that the man inside had started to play the piano; and he was *very* good indeed at playing it.

Shannon waited near the end of the wall by the fence for Grandad and 'Tuppence to come out the front door. She heard them laughing as they came out and they creaked the door closed behind them. The piano could still be heard inside. She peered round the corner to see Grandad's pipe blowing clouds of smoke around him as they chatted. She was getting *really* cold now and was so uncomfortable. She heard Grandad say to Uncle Tuppence "Come on then, let's get going." and they started to walk the other way from her, in the direction of Grandad's house. She began to worry that Grandad would get home soon and check on her in her room, only to find her pile of pillows lying in her bed instead of Shannon. Her mind raced, trying to think of another route to take to get ahead of them as she followed on quietly, far behind. But she needn't have worried. They turned right, opening the gate of the church. "What on earth are they *doing*", she thought?

She crept slowly behind and saw them go round the back of the church hall and soon walk back to the front door of the church with a long wooden ladder between them. She'd seen the ladder before, as Grandad used it for painting high windows and signs when he was working. Shannon was amazed when she saw Grandad take a key from his pocket and open up the church door, before they struggled in through the doors of it with the ladder. She leapt up on the side wall next to the church to try to see what they were doing in the church through the high windows. They knew not to put any lights on, but a small red lamp was on at the side of the altar, which gave Shannon just enough light to see that they had gone right through the church and up towards the altar. She couldn't see that far, so she crept down off the wall and back round to the door of the church, before silently creeping in. Crouching, she hid behind the back row of seats, hardly daring to breathe in case she was discovered. It was dark, but her eyes soon let her see the pinkish glow of Grandad and Uncle Tuppence, thanks to that small red lamp. High above the altar on the back wall was a big, decorative thing, which looked like a huge, wooden, sticking out balcony. Mum had told her before that it was called a 'baldequino'. Shannon always laughed that the name sounded like a baldy-queen to her! She saw them lift the ladder and place it way high up against the side of it. Tuppence held the ladder at the bottom as Grandad started to climb. Shannon suddenly heard the door at the side of the altar open and saw the old priest, Father Davis appear. Grandad stopped, half way up. "Oh-oh!" thought Shannon "they're in trouble now, they've been *caught!*"

She expected Father Davis to start shouting at them. But no, in fact he seemed very happy to see them, joking "Take it easy up there Jimmy!" and "A fine night for it tonight gentlemen!" The more Shannon saw and heard, the more confusing this night got! Father Davis turned his head to look up at Grandad, who climbed higher and higher, until he reached the top of the baldequino. He grunted as he stretched over the top, like he was trying to grab something. "It never gets any easier with time, does it Jimmy?" Father Davis joked up to Grandad. Tuppence giggled at the bottom of the ladder. "Got it!" said Grandad.

"Careful now!" said Tuppence, turning to look up and taking his holding foot off the bottom of the ladder, making it wobble. "No, *you* be careful Tuppence! Hold that blooming ladder still!" cursed Grandad from above. There was no laughter now, as Tuppence quickly grabbed the ladder and steadied it again. Grandad had obviously got something very precious and important from up there. He cradled that small something inside his jacket, letting himself gently down the ladder with the other hand, step by step. At last he was down and the three men gathered round each other on the altar. Shannon tried as hard as she could to see what it was that they had. It was so silent in that pink glow down there. She couldn't quite see, but it looked to Shannon like some sort of a tin. Grandad's elbow came up and a screech came out from the tin as he slowly unscrewed the metal lid. A few more turns and Shannon gradually saw Grandad's face light up in a beautiful golden glow rise from the tin as he looked inside. At the same time, a beautiful ray of light the same golden colour streamed from the painting right above her at the church door, across to the stained glass window behind and right down the church to the tin in Grandad's hand! The three men just stood just staring inside for a few seconds, until Grandad slowly put the lid back on and the ray of light disappeared. "I'd best get going" said Grandad. They shook Father Davis' hand, thanked him and wished him goodnight. But Shannon's eyes opened wide with panic as they then turned to walk towards her down the aisle of the church. She scrambled herself towards the door on her knees in the dark and nudged it open, squeezing through the gap. She stood up and opened the next door and ran out into the cold night air again before crouching down behind a big bush in the garden. A few seconds later Grandad and Tuppence quietly crept out of the door. "No! Must've just been the wind that caught the door." She heard Tuppence say to Grandad, as he locked the door behind him. She watched them through the leaves of the bush, trying to hold her breath to stay quiet. They swung the squeaking church gate behind them and turned not towards home, but back again towards the town. For a second Shannon was relieved. At least she could now get back to Grandad's house before he did and not get caught for being out at night. But after seeing all this, how could she go home now without knowing what's happening? More questions raced into her mind: What was that stuff in the tin? Why was it up there? What had Father Davis to do with it? Why was it all so secretive, in the dark, in the middle of the night? Why has Grandad got a key to the church…and where were they going now? "Right!" she thought, as she scrambled out of the bush "I've so many questions here. I'm going to try and get them answered! "

She waited for a couple of minutes, then followed Grandad and Tuppence down the road. Expecting them to just go back to the community centre after passing the bus-station, she was surprised when they turned left instead, along the tree-lined road towards the museum. She followed on, working her way along the trees as hiding places. They walked past the big statue of a doctor and behind the museum. There were lots of big, dark bushes for Shannon to hide behind, so she could get quite close. She watched through the dark leaves as Grandad took out a key and opened the door to a large shed, which was joined to the museum and stepped inside. She waited for what seemed like hours in that cold, bug-filled darkness for them to come back out. She was about to give up and go back to Grandad's house when suddenly she heard the shed doors slowly creak and wisps of white smoke blew out through the gap between them! It was pretty silent from the shed up to now, but suddenly there was some noise. A lot of shuffling and banging about, followed by a moan obviously from Grandad "That was my *foot*, thank you very much!" and "Watch it...careful now!" A few seconds later a long, low, mechanical *Hiiiiisssssssssssssss*, like a small steam train and then a couple more small bangs. All this was then followed by a couple of loud, throaty coughs that were *definitely* Grandads! He seemed to be coughing a lot these days.

Finally there was another small bang as the door nearest to Shannon shook and swung open as a wave of golden light streamed out across the park. Besides the surprise, Shannon was amazed at seeing so much light at night again, for the first time in years! But the golden glow quickly faded away until it was almost dark again. Shannon couldn't see inside, the open door was blocking her way. But she could hear. "You sure that you've got everything there Jimmy?" asked Tuppence. "Yes, everything's here, stop worrying, man!" Shannon stared as she heard the two struggling to push something out of the shed. First to appear was a shiny, spoked wheel, moving very slowly forwards out of the shed. Then...yes, some handlebars, with Grandad's arms pushing them. She was disappointed when she realised it must just be Grandad's bike. But why were they struggling so much with it? Grandad is pretty ancient now, but he was a boxer when he was young and always kept himself pretty fit for his age. But as more of the bike appeared she realised why it was so heavy. Just behind Grandad, attached to the bike were two huge, white, feathered wings! As more of the bike appeared she saw a large wooden box– trailer at the back of the bike, covered in a blanket, which was held down by rope. Now this night was getting just plain crazy!

She was dying to rush out and ask Grandad and Tuppence all about this, but she also knew that she'd be in major trouble for being out at night, so she stayed hidden by the bushes. She could only think that maybe the reason that Grandad put these huge wings and trailer on his bike was to prepare it for the end of summer parade up the High Street – but why now, in December?

Shannon heard Tuppence mention to Grandad that he'd left something upstairs in the museum and that he'd be "back soon". She watched Grandad on his own, putting on his flat-cap and tucking his tweed trousers neatly into his socks. He stood with his hands on his hips, staring quietly and happily into the night sky above him. He looked so peaceful and so content with everything. But Shannon felt that she *had* to get closer to see that bike and quickly, because 'Tuppence would be down again soon. Grandad walked a few steps across the grass onto the park for a quick stroll, still staring up at the night sky. This was Shannon's chance! She quietly crept out of the bushes, staying low and quietly raced across the grass towards the bike. She got to the back wheel nearest her and crouched down, the huge, white, feathered wings above her. Suddenly she heard Tuppence moving about behind her. He must be coming back. Time to hide!

Panicking, she stood up, pulled back a bit of blanket on the box trailer and quietly climbed inside, pulling the loose flap down behind her. It was pitch black in there, but comfortable. The trailer seemed to only have some soft cloths and a few other small things in there, so there was plenty of room for her inside. She stayed so still though as Tuppence talked to Grandad right above her: "All right Jimmy. I think that's you all set to go then."

Where could Grandad be going? And on *this* weird looking thing, after midnight? He could hardly get far in this thing. She thought of waiting to find a way to sneak back out of the box and go home, but how could she without being seen? Suddenly, Shannon almost leapt up out of the trailer-box with fright as Tuppence slapped its' side "You're pretty sure that you put the big tin and the dusters in the trailer here?" Shannon was relieved at Grandad's reply from the front of the bike. "For Goodness' sakes Tuppence, how many times have you asked about that? Y*es, it's all in there!"* he chuckled.

"And you've got the wee jar in your jacket pocket?" replied Tuppence. Shannon didn't hear Grandad answer, so figured out that he must have shown him that he had it. Tuppence's brushing steps on the grass could be heard as he walked away round to the front of the bike towards Grandad. She dared to push a piece of the blanket above her up and peek out, looking through the gap. She saw Grandad stepping off the bike and reach into his jacket pocket. He took out a small jar and started to screw it open. Could it be what Grandad had at the church tonight, she thought? She soon knew it must be, as the jar lid was slowly taken off and that golden glow appeared around it again just like earlier. Grandad smiled, looked up at the sky and then dipped his finger into the jar. He took it out, covered again in the most beautiful, flowing gold that Shannon had ever seen. He walked round to one of the huge, feathered wings and gently brushed his fingers over the tips of the feathers. To Shannon's amazement, every feather on the wing suddenly glowed a brilliant white! He went to the other wing, near Tuppence and it did the same. She felt a slight movement on the bike and she realised that the wings were very slowly starting to move...up...and down....! *How* was Grandad making that happen? 'Pretty impressive!' She thought. 'He's put so much work into this, just for a summer parade? Surely not!' She was frightened and excited, all at the same time. What could she do? There was no chance of risking jumping out the back into the darkness and getting seen by Grandad and Tuppence, or she'd end up in real trouble. Instead she should maybe stay here. Maybe she'd end up getting banged about and perhaps even hurt in the back of the trailer on any bumpy roads that Grandad might go on? But she decided to stay. At least that way she'd hopefully find out just what's going on.

The wings started to flap slightly quicker and she could hear them gently whistling as they blew up and down. "All right, have a good trip Jimmy. And say hello to Himself from me." Tuppence said, as he tapped Grandad on the back. Tuppence stood back and the wings started to beat harder and faster. Grandad turned his cap back to front, grabbed some flying goggles from the handlebars of the bike and slipped them on. The bike started to move forwards, as Grandad raised himself and pushed down on the pedals. He turned it right and pedalled harder, across the rough grass. Shannon started to feel every bump as the bike started to speed up and was seriously worried now that she was going to get badly hurt if this went on much longer. The wings thumped and flapped up and down, faster by the second. The blanket above her started to flap about loudly too, thundering like a rolling drum. The bike raced quicker and quicker across the bumpy grass. Shannon was bounced about harder and in the box as they rattled along. She held on in all that noise and jumping about and managed to peek out of the side. They were heading straight for that line of big trees and the edge of the hill! She peeked ahead, terrified in all that shaking and bumping! Grandad didn't seem to be slowing down at all. The wings were flapping so quickly. The trees were so close now! But then the bumping suddenly stopped and with a smooth WHOOOSH........*up* they went into the night sky!

Chapter 4 – To The Stars

Shannon was thrown into the back of the box as the bike and trailer tipped and rose into the air, but pulled herself back up to open a peephole in the blanket to see out. She held on so tight, but could only look out in utter amazement as she saw the trees, museum and whole park shrink below her as she flew up into the dark blue night sky! The breeze flapped her hair around her face, but all that could really be heard was the slower, whooshing flapping of the wings and the night breeze. She then noticed the sea appear below her, the darkest blue with shimmering yellow sparkles. The roofs of the houses near the beach reflected some of the moon's bright glow as the town slowly shrunk into the distance far below them. She turned in the box and pulled herself to the front to peek out. The shadowy, peaceful looking figure of Grandad in front of her, pedalling away slowly, with moonlight glow around him, gliding up into the night sky with those magical flapping wings beside him was so incredible. She knew that she should be terrified, climbing so high with these whooshing rushes of wind, flapping blanket and the cold night air. But seeing Grandad looking so calm on this incredible thing, moving smoothly up into such a beautiful night sky only made her feel so happy, safe and proud. She now knew that it *wasn't* all just a story…it was *all real*!

Up and up they went, past the few clouds that slept lazily in the skies that night. Soon she could see the mountains and the islands so far away, down to her left surrounded by the moonlit, sparkling sea. The sky grew darker and darker. The town was now gone, somewhere amongst all that darkness down there. She began to panic. It was getting harder to

31

breathe up here and getting *so* cold! She looked ahead towards Grandad's back as he pedalled. She'd have to tell him she was there soon, no matter what trouble she'd get into! She opened up the peephole in the blanket further and nervously started to reach forward to tap his back and get his attention. But something suddenly stopped her. She saw Grandad reach into his jacket again and dip his finger into the pot, as her hand just reached the springs under the bike seat. He flicked his glowing finger into the air above him and wonderful, golden dust sprinkled all over the bike. Straight away the feathered wings suddenly seemed to grow even larger and changed from white to that brilliant, wonderful gold. Incredibly, the coldness suddenly went and she was suddenly warm; and the breeze and drumming of the blanket flapping had stopped altogether! And what's more, she could breath probably better than she ever could! Whatever that dust was it seemed to make everything alright.

She looked around her. It was so, so peaceful now, so beautiful. She relaxed in the box, her feet sticking out of the back to allow her to see the fantastic views. They had soared up so high now. Suddenly she smiled with excitement as she noticed the curve of the earth. That made her think of her school project and the pictures of space in her schoolbook. If only her teacher could see this! The Earth slowly turned into a dark ball, with the most beautiful whites, blues and greens swirling around one side – like the fanciest glass marble she could imagine.

She amazed herself by not being afraid right then, but then, Grandad being here made everything all right. She looked down at The Earth and picked out where France and Belgium were. She immediately thought of her Daddy and blew him a kiss, knowing he was down there somewhere. She touched her forehead with her finger, just as Daddy had taught her, to always know that he was with her. She so wished he could see her. He'd be *so* proud, so amazed. As she stared down and thought all of these things she hardly noticed that the sky all around them was now pitch black, with thousands of stars to break it all up. She had no idea how fast they were going, it all seemed so relaxed and still. The only sound was the gentle, slow flapping of those beautiful, glowing wings. But she also knew that they must be going very fast indeed, because the earth seemed to be getting smaller and smaller by the minute. She quietly went to the front of the box again and was shocked to see the moon ahead of them so absolutely huge and quickly getting closer and closer. She began to see dusty hills and huge craters on its surface. Soon they were almost touching it. 'Oh my goodness!' thought Shannon – we're actually going to land on the moon!'

They were so close to landing now – no higher than her school bell-tower from the dusty ground. The huge wings stopped flapping and they glided slowly down. She looked around and saw her latest strange sight of the night. It can't be! There ahead was a small house, on the moon, with a beautiful, grassy garden, full of blooming flowers and a small fence all around it! As they glided slowly down towards it Shannon could see an old man standing at the front door, happily waving up at them! But instead of landing they swooped past, so close to the roof. Grandad waved to the man and threw down a rolled up newspaper to him, which landed at the man's feet. As they passed she heard the man below shouting up "Thanks Jimmy, I'll get the kettle on then!" and laughing. Without thinking, Shannon then automatically waved down to the old man from the trailer herself, before she realised she maybe should have stayed hidden. She watched the old man's wave slow down, as though he was worried. Shannon looked forwards again towards Grandad, who seemed to be making sure that his goggles and cap were on correctly once more. He put his head down and forward over the handlebars. The great wings started to flap harder than ever, as they flew back up into space, faster than ever. Shannon could now see over Grandad's shoulders in front of her. She noticed thin, silvery lines reaching off in lots of directions far into space. The wings suddenly stopped flapping and tucked themselves in tight to the sides of the bike. A few seconds later, when they seemed to have reached one of the silvery lines, Shannon was thrown back again into the back of the box. She gasped as the bike raced forward at a terrific speed! She waited a few seconds, but pulled herself back to see out the front again. Sure enough, the bike was travelling along one of those silvery lines. Whatever they were, they were making the bike travel *so* quickly! Looking over Grandad's shoulders she saw that their line seemed to be taking them directly towards a twinkling star. This was incredible enough, but what really got her was the incredible, warm, glowing colour of the star ahead. She'd never seen a colour like it before. If she tried to explain the colour to anyone, she wouldn't be able to, as it was like no colour on earth. All she could do was stare ahead as they went towards it. She couldn't help herself "Woooooooww!" she gasped! Grandad quickly turned round and Shannon dived under the blanket, only her heartbeat thumping in her ears. 'Did he see me?' she thought. Nothing happened, so she must have got away with it! She stayed under the trailer cover, hiding.

Soon she felt the bike slowing down, but she didn't dare look out right now. As they came to a stop, she slowly felt such a lovely, growing, glowing, almost *tickly* feeling all over her body. It was a wonderful feeling though, like when Mum hugged her, but like getting a thousand hugs at once! Soon she felt the bike gently shaking and it felt like Grandad had got off the bike! She just had to look out. Her hand poked a tiny peephole in the side of the blanket and a fantastic light streamed in. She looked out

34

and all she could see was that bright, glowing star-colour – but *everywhere*! It was so fantastically bright, but amazingly never hurt her eyes at all. She opened the peephole wider and looked forward. There was Grandad, a dark shadow against the bright light, standing on the silvery thread at the front of his bike. And in front of him, not much taller than him and *right* next to them - was the *star*! Grandad's hand went forward and slowly stroked the fantastic, warm light. He looked so happy and peaceful. "Hello folks, how are you tonight?" he said to the star, which puzzled Shannon. He turned and walked towards the trailer box, still smiling – right towards Shannon! She suddenly panicked as his hands started to untie the ropes and the blanket above her, as he pulled it towards the back of the trailer box. Oh no! she thought. This is it, I'm caught now! She was right. Suddenly a mighty gasp of shock came out from Grandad as he stared down at her. "*Shannon*! What are you doing here?" She gulped. She was in *real* trouble now!

Chapter 5 – Secret Cleaning

Shannon didn't know what to say. Grandad just leant forward onto the side of the trailer box and held his hands to his face, shaking his head in shock and wondering what to do next. He looked up through his fingers to look at her, in shock. She saw that he looked so worried and before long he started to ask her lots of questions:

"Does your Granny know you're out? How did you find out about the museum? How did you get into the box? How much did you see? How much do you know?"

Shannon would hate to tell her beloved Grandad a lie and so she told him everything – about sneaking out of Granny's house, following him to the 'Centre, the church, the museum, sneaking in, the lot! As she told him, he just kept shaking his head, like he was getting more and more disappointed, the more he heard.

"You should never have followed me tonight Shannon".

She reached up to him and touched his arm, she didn't want to see him being disappointed with her.

"But Grandad – if you'd never told me about cleaning the stars – if you hadn't made me wonder if it was all true, I would never have found out! And you've asked me lots of questions, I've seen so many amazing things tonight that I can't explain, I've got a *million* questions that I could ask you!"

For the first time tonight, Grandad nodded "I suppose so Shannon. Bit I also suppose that I just hoped that you would have thought that it was all a big story. I wanted it to be just that – a magical story for you. I should have just kept my big mouth shut, but I so love that look in your eyes when you hear stories about 'magic' things. Right now, you're one of only a very few who know the truth. Not even your Granny knows that this is all true!"

He reached down, gently lifted her out of the box-trailer and stood her on the silvery threads, right next to the star! She gasped at how beautiful it looked again and how fantastic and 'glowy' it made her feel! Granddad saw her look down, she felt so safe, but her feet were only on that very thin, silvery thread! "It's all right Shannon, you can't fall in space, trust me!" he smiled. Shannon wanted to know more.

"But Grandad, why keep it all a secret? It's such a wonderful thing. I mean, going to the *stars* Grandad! *All this*, f*or real*!" Shannon said, excitedly looking all around her.

Grandad stared at Shannon and was quiet for a while, and sighed before answering.

"Because no-one would believe it Shannon! Most people just want to believe in what the world, the newspapers and the people around them want them to believe. Most people just want to fit in, without thinking for themselves. So few people look deep inside themselves to know what's actually true. And what's worse, so many people laugh at those who do bother to believe in what they feel deep inside. Your Granny is a wonderful woman and I love her eternally, more than words can *ever* say. But she's been too long in the world to believe enough to even come with me to see for herself. When your Mother was a little girl and I told her about cleaning stars, she had the same look of belief in her eye that you do". Grandad leaned down to look Shannon in the face.

"And why would we take just anyone up here anyway? Would they respect and love the stars? Or would many just ruin them and take away their magic? Just make them into some kind of, I don't know - circus attraction? Shannon, do you know that every single little baby is born knowing inside what's absolutely true? They believe and know what's true so absolutely perfectly. And the world just eats it slowly away from them as they start to grow! But telling people what you believe is true can be very brave, but can end in disaster. When your Mother was a wee girl and told the others at school about it she was teased, just like you were Shannon."

Shannon looked up, remembering Veronica and her horrible laughter.

"In one way, I was so proud that you and your Mother believed so much in the stars that you were brave enough to tell others about it all. But I was also so incredibly sad when you got laughed at for it. I felt terrible! So I kept it to look like just a wonderful story. I mean, how could I *not* tell the people that mean more than the whole universe to me about all *this*? It's a strange thing, but adults sometimes try to make up stories and pretend that they're real. But here am I, telling you about something real and trying to pretend it's a story!" he smiled.

Grandad put his hand on her shoulder as he turned her gently round beside him to look back towards the Earth, with that beautiful, swirling, blue, green and white edge. They just stood there, admiring the view of it, swirling away in the distance. His arm went down over her shoulder as she hugged him tightly. She looked up and saw him smiling down at her, but his eyes full of tears. "Oh Grandad, what's the matter?" she asked, concerned. "Oh, don't you worry Shannon, I'm just so proud of you for being so brave, for being up here with me to see all this – but mostly, for *believing*!" With that a green "whoooooosssshhh" of light flew past, right in front of them! Grandad laughed as Shannon had ducked down beside the bike. "Oh don't worry Shannon, it's just a shooting star, you'll get used to them! Come on then, you didn't come up here for nothing - grab yourself a couple of cloths from the trailer box then, we've got some work to do!"

Shannon went back to the trailer box and took out two cloths. Now that the starlight lit up the whole of the box, she was puzzled at how little there was in there, just two cloths, two or three little bags, some tins of paint and some brushes. She passed Grandad the cloths, but he handed one back.

"Are you not helping then?" he smiled.

He leaned down towards her again. Shannon stared at the glowing gold shine of the star right next to her though and wondered what she was supposed to do.

"Grandad, I don't mean to be funny, but this star is the most beautiful, shiny, perfect thing I've ever seen. How can I make something so beautiful any cleaner?" He laughed.

"You're absolutely right Shannon! There's no way that a wee cloth and our working on a star can possibly make it look any shinier, or glow any harder. But then, we're not here to actually make it *look* cleaner..."

He could see that Shannon didn't understand.

"We're here to *care* for the stars Shannon, to show them that they're loved and that we remember them and appreciate that they shine down on us. If we don't do that, how are they supposed to know that people down there on Earth care? How would they shine?" Now she looked *really* confused.

"Look Shannon, imagine if I was to do one of two things – either to wash your face with a facecloth, *or* to give you a hug and tell you a story. Which of the two would make you feel really good *inside*, hmm?"

"The story of course!" she smiled.

"Absolutely! Well, it's the same with stars Shannon. We're here to *help* them glow by letting them know how *loved* they are! I use cloths just to wipe the love into them. Now a facecloth can make your skin glow a tiny bit better for a tiny bit of time. It's an important thing to do, of course. But it only cleans you for a *wee* while and only on the *outside*! But a hug and a story can *really* make you glow! It's the *love* in that hug and story that lasts forever. Look around - the stars, the moon, the Earth down there. All of this can only really be here because of love. One day you'll understand just how important these stars are – and *what* they are! But now isn't the time for that."

She knew Grandad well enough to know that he meant what he said. She also knew that it wasn't really worth asking him any more about why the stars are so important. But she did ask anyway "Grandad, if we're here to pass love to the stars and clean them 'inside', how do we know when the star's finished?"

Grandad turned to her again and nodded "Now that's a very, very good question Shannon. All I can say right now is that you'll know yourself when it's finished." He gently grabbed her arm which was holding the cloth "And you'll never find out when a star's finished unless you begin one, now will you!" She was so excited. Grandad turned towards the star, holding her hand next to him. He lifted his hand gently and slowly moved it into the light. As he did so, a beautiful sprinkling of golden dust blew out of the star and drifted slowly out into space around them. "That dust!" said Shannon, so excited "It's what you have in that tin in the church, isn't it?" He grinned and winked "It could well be Shannon! Now, your turn.Think wonderful thoughts Shannon, of any nice memories that you have, maybe a Christmas Day with Mum, baking with Granny, anything you like." She closed her eyes and thought of a wonderful day that she had on the beach with Mum, Dad, Granny and Grandad, tucking into ice-creams from Maranti's sweet shop; the sun beaming down and seagulls soaring high above them. She felt a wide smile grow across her face, then opened her eyes. Grandad slowly lifted her hand into the light. The golden dust blew out of the star towards her and she felt the most wonderful, incredible happiness wash over her, like a thousand beach days with ice-cream rolled into one! And the weirdest thing of all was that here she was, far out into space, with the earth glowing far behind them – and she had never felt so at home before! They stood silently side by side, faces glowing and wonderful, golden dust dancing in space around them. She noticed Grandad catching the dust in that jar in his jacket pocket. "What are you collecting that for Grandad?" He kept looking forward, catching the dust "Well, without this wonderful stuff, we can't fly up here Shannon, we'd be stuck down there!" he nodded backwards towards the Earth.

After a few minutes Shannon noticed the star suddenly grow slightly warmer. She brought her hand down by her side and looked at Grandad, who only smiled knowingly. Something started to change in the star. She could see something appear right in front of her, deep in the star. The shape of a beautiful face, looking warmly at her! Rather than being scared she just kept staring. It had the most wonderful smile and the smile was moving! Suddenly the most wonderful singing that Shannon had ever heard came from it, which seemed to be filling the whole of space around them, making her head tingle. She never said a word, just kept staring at this beautiful face and listening to that wonderful song. She didn't know why, but she knew inside that the song was for her. Happy tears ran down her face at how beautiful and peaceful it all was. Soon the singing stopped and that beautiful, golden face just kept looking out at her, with the most wonderful smile. Shannon wiped her tears on her sleeve, but kept staring into the star. She jumped slightly as a glowing, golden hand and arm slowly came out of the face, gently stroking her cheek. "Don't be afraid Shannon!" whispered the face, with such love; as her cheek tingled against the glowing hand. "And thank you for being here". The glowing hand reached down to hers and gently lifted it to touch the star again. Slowly she felt and saw the hand and face disappear into the star again, leaving her feeling more peaceful and happy than she thought anyone could ever be, still staring into the star. She suddenly turned to Grandad, like waking up "Well Shannon" smiled Grandad "that's one star finished!"

She just stood there, staring into the star and gasped "*Who* was that beautiful woman in the star Grandad?"

"An angel Shannon, an angel!"

She turned and stared all around her – whispering "An angel!" to herself, amazed at what a night it had been. Grandad reached for his cap, and got on his bike "Come on then Shannon. Take your cloth and get in the box-trailer, we've lots more of these to do!" He moved the bike so that the front wheel was over another silvery line, which pointed to another star in the far distance. Shannon got in and Grandad passed her a spare pair of goggles for her eyes. She looked down "What exactly are these silvery lines we're on Grandad? Are they something magical too, maybe some kind of angel's hair, or starry rope or something?" He laughed" No Shannon, they're just spider's webs! The spiders that get caught up in strong winds and end up being carried up here from Earth make them for me, to help me find my way around easier! Just because we might see something every day, such as a spider, and we're used to seeing it, it doesn't make it any less magical!"

He reached into his pocket and threw some golden stardust into space above them. "All right Shannon, 'you ready? Hold *on!*" The great wings started to flap and Shannon's laughed out loud as her tummy tickled as they suddenly *whoooooooshed* so quickly along those silvery webs towards the next star!

It was like the most wonderful dream. They went from star to glowing star on those silvery webs, way up in glittering space. The angels' singing from inside the stars never got any less beautiful and the stardust never got any less amazing in its beautiful colour and sparkle. Grandad let her collect some in the jar and when she looked in and gently moved the jar, it moved like a wonderful, liquid golden sunset. Grandad showed her a map that he'd drawn in pencil of the stars that they had to clean and care for that night. What amazed her was that when they'd finished a star, the drawing of it on the paper magically disappeared on its own! He told her that he got the information about which stars need to be cleaned from the black dome in the Community Centre that she'd seen earlier through the window.

"How does the information get into the globe Grandad?" she asked.
But there were some things that even Grandad couldn't answer, *or* maybe wanted to be kept secret! He was just told that the angels put it there and that was that. They finished the last star. Shannon looked at the drawing and saw it disappear, leaving just a blank piece of paper in her hand.

"Right then! That's us finished Shannon! Well done and thanks for the help." Grandad grinned. She was disappointed that it was all over, after seeing those wonderful, glowing stars, that beautiful singing, those angel's faces.
"One stop left and then we're heading home!" he said, pulling on his goggles again.

Shannon's face lit up – still something amazing to do tonight!

"Great! Where to now then Grandad?" she asked excitedly.

He reached into his pocket and brought out a small, white ball and threw it to her "Catch!" She caught it. "Emmm, a golf-ball! Thanks Grandad, but what's this for?"

"Well, we're off to the moon, of course. We'd better take a few spare balls or it's not fair on Angus there if we keep using his!" Shannon was once again absolutely puzzled. She was going to ask Grandad what on earth he meant, but he was already leaping onto the bike and reaching into his pocket again. He stopped and turned round to her. "Well? Are you getting in or what Shannon?"

"Oh…right!" she said, as she clambered into the trailer-box again. Grandad put his feet down and moved the bike round onto a silvery web that stretched far away, straight back to the moon. "Ready Shannon?" he yelled over his shoulder. "Ready Granddad" she screamed.

He threw some stardust up into space above her again, which sparkled all around them as the glowing wings flapped, racing them forward – *to the moon*!

Chapter 6 – The Man on the Moon

The moon grew closer and closer, until it filled the whole of space in front of them. Soon she could see that house again, the one that she'd seen as they'd whooshed by earlier. The flapping of the wings slowed down, until they glided them gently down towards landing. Grandad turned round to her, his face covered in the stardust that he's thrown up earlier, his goggles wiped clean of it with finger-marks. "Hold on Shannon, this might be a bit bumpy!" he shouted. They were so close to the ground now and Shannon could see the man from earlier through a window in his house, seeing them and getting up as they flashed by. The wings tipped and they swung round the house, then flapped strongly forwards, acting like brakes and slowing them down. Grandad shouted out to duck under the covers in the box trailer, as they were in for a dusty landing! The wheels of the bike and trailer touched down on the grey, powdery ground and they bumped along in a cloud of flying moon-dust, with the wings flapping backwards harder then ever, until they came to a dusty, coughing stop!

Shannon peeped out again and through the powdery air she could see the man opening his garden gate and starting to walk towards them. He was dressed just like most other old men she'd seen back home – white shirt, jacket and black trousers. He had wisps of white hair and a cheery old face. "You all right?" said Grandad. She turned forwards to look at him and immediately burst out laughing. He was *covered* in grey, powdery moon-dust and looked like a talking statue! He brushed himself down with his hands and turned to look over his shoulder towards the old man, who was almost at the bike.

"How are you tonight Angus?" shouted Grandad to the man. The man laughed "Oh…yes! I'm fine thanks Jimmy. The man pointed at him, laughing "Bit of a dusty landing tonight then?"

He turned his head, with a lovely smile on his face "And you must be Shannon!" and gently shook her hand.

Grandad nodded towards them "Yes, this is Shannon Angus, she sneaked into the trailer back at the museum shed."

"Yes" grinned Angus "I got a nice wee wave from the trailer on the way past earlier and I thought it must be Shannon. You gave me quite a shock! But not to worry my dear, you're here now and that's that." he smiled down at her.

She wondered how he knew her name, and opened her mouth to ask. But her words were stopped as he took a bottle from behind his back and handed it to her, saying

"I believe that this is your favourite drink, Shannon – sugarelly?"

"Thank you!" she grinned!

"My pleasure Shannon, my name's Angus, by the way. But if you want to call me Uncle, I'd be very honoured."

He helped Shannon out of the box-trailer. She stepped down onto the white, rocky surface and suddenly thought "I'm on the *moon*!"

So many amazing things had happened to her that night that almost nothing seemed to surprise her now. She took his hand as they all wandered towards his house. As they walked Shannon wondered not just how an old man could live on the moon, but also how an old man knew about sugarelly! She thought that only children knew about it, or at least bothered to make it.

Angus looked over his shoulder and laughed out loudly as Grandad followed on, thumping his jacket clean in a cloud of moon-dust. Shannon kept looking forward though. *What* an amazing sight! A beautiful, flowery, fenced garden in front of her, surrounding a lovely little cottage – on the moon! And there in the far distance, floating in space was The Earth! Angus opened the gate and held it open for Shannon.

"After you!"

As she walked through the gate, Shannon suddenly thought to herself that she was sure that she'd seen him somewhere before, but then she heard him and Grandad laughing and wrestling about behind her.

"Jimmy! Quit it!"

Angus laughed, as Grandad tried to wipe as much moon-dust from his shoulders onto him as possible. He giggled and half-tried to get away, almost falling over the gate, as Grandad rubbed some moon-dust into his head. Angus saw Shannon looking and straightened himself up, like he suddenly remembered that he had to act like a responsible adult now! What didn't help was that he was also now covered in moon-dust and the bits of white hair that he had were sticking up like twisted dry grass! He pulled his jacket straight, coughed some dust out of his mouth, smoothed his hair down and walked past Shannon to the open the door, Grandad grinning away closely behind him.

Shannon walked into the house. It was just like many other houses, a bit like Grandad's really. There was a coat-stand on the way in, a stairway, a sitting room with a roaring fire and some chairs, and a kitchen through the back. But the one thing that no other house anywhere had was the view from the living room window – the surface of the moon beyond the garden and the whole Earth itself as a background, with the occasional shooting star whooshing by! Grandad went through to the bathroom to clean himself up, as 'Uncle' Angus' invited Shannon to sit at the table by the window. He got a glass out for her "For your sugarelly." he smiled "I'll get the pot heated up again for some tea for your Grandad and me – back soon!" he winked, as he left the room. She shook up the sugarelly in the bottle and poured the frothy, brown mix into the glass, where it foamed like a sweet volcano. She could see and taste that Angus made a wonderful sugarelly – for an old man! And like everyone does when they're suddenly alone in a new house, she sat and looked around the room. There were lots of interesting things. Medals, a soldier's cap, a few horse ornaments. There was even an old football on the far end of the mantelpiece over the fireplace, which had *'Sandy McNeil, Ypres, 24/12/1914'* written on it in pen. This seemed pretty strange to Shannon. 'Imagine putting a football on display over a fireplace, she thought.

But then what really caught Shannon's eye was a painting higher up above the fireplace. She got up and walked across to it for a closer look. It was a lovely looking painting of a castle on some rocks out on the sea. *'What a great looking place for a castle'*, she thought. But then something caught her eye in the picture. In the sea by the castle was a long wooden boat with a sail. It seemed strange to her, but she thought that she'd seen the boat somewhere before. But then the most incredible thing happened. The more that she looked at the boat in the painting, the more she thought that she actually saw it *move*. She stared at it, then jumped. Yes – it *moved*! But even more incredible, she then found that if her eyes looked at another place in the painting, the boat moved to where she looked. She just *had* to reach up and touch the painting and stretched up on her tiptoes, almost burning herself against the fire-guard. She got a fright and turned round quickly as Grandad came back into the room. "It *is* a lovely painting, isn't it Shannon?" he said, as he sat down at the table. She stood there, looking over at him.

"Grandad, I know that this is going to sound daft, but I could have sworn that the boat in that painting….moves!". She blushed with embarrassment as she said it, imagining how strange it must have sounded!

But Grandad's eyes opened wide, like something amazing had happened! "What did you say Shannon?" like he didn't quite believe what she said. She felt even more silly, like she must have imagined the boat moving, but she quietly said it again.

He got up, so excited and raced over to the fireplace, grabbing the painting from the wall and held it up in front of her. "Please Shannon" he asked quickly *"Show* me – make the boat move" She was worried now. She could see that Grandad *really* wanted to see her move the boat in the picture, but maybe she just imagined it. She didn't want to let him down or look like a fool! Anyway, she started to stare straight at the boat, not expecting much to happen, but wanting it *so* much. Then she moved her eyes to look at the sea on the other side of the castle in the painting…and the boat followed!

Grandad excitedly placed the painting gently back above the fireplace, turned round and cried *"Yyyyyyyyyeeeesssss!"* throwing his arms in the air and then lifting Shannon up. He spun her round and hugged her so tightly! She looked down at him as they spun round. He had the widest smile, with the happiest tears in his eyes. She was so glad that she made the boat move, but what did it all mean?

Angus came through from the kitchen, two cups of tea in his hands and asked "What's going on?"

Grandad smiled at him "Listen Angus, if I were you, I'd put those cups down before I tell you!" As Angus did, he told him what Shannon had done and he was almost as happy as Grandad was! "Well done Shannon!" he grinned, tapping her back. She loved the attention, but was amazed and puzzled at how happy they both were about this!

Grandad looked straight at her, still up in his arms, so happy and said "Well, well, well Shannon. I thought that it was just bad luck that you sneaked into the box-trailer and came up here tonight, but you're *meant* to be here.The angels wanted it! They chose *you!*"
He could see that Shannon wondered what he meant.
"Come on and sit down by the table Shannon".
They all sat. Angus gently took the painting from the fireplace and laid it flat on the table in front of them. Grandad leaned across the table at Shannon
"I'd best explain" he said.
"Shannon, the boat and the castle in the picture are *very* special to our family. Now as far as we know the painting was done by the angels themselves. Our ancestors came from far away to a lovely, special island in that very boat shown in the picture, about a thousand years ago. The island is quite small and far, far out to sea. But they found that the island 'felt' special to them, even though it could get cold and stormy. It had wonderful beaches, rocky pools, mountains and was surrounded by greeny-blue seas filled with seals, whales, dolphins, sharks, the odd mermaid or two and millions of tasty fish. They liked it so much and it felt so good to be there, that they stayed. At the bottom end of the island was a big bay, perfect to make a harbour for boats, protecting them from wild storms. And in that bay, quite far out was a tinier island, not much bigger

than your school playground. Strangely, they found that it had a fresh water spring full of beautiful drinking water in it. So they built their castle there. They lived there in that castle for many hundreds of years, until not too long ago. Some of our ancestors also had the secret job of caring for the stars, that no-one else in the family knew about. They were secretly called 'Starcarers'. They needed their little supply of stardust to allow them to get up here too, just like us. So, they hid a box of stardust in a secret cave under the castle. So the castle was built on that little island there not only to keep our ancestors safe, but it also turned out to be an excellent and safe hiding place for the Starcarers to put their secret stardust in. I've been told that our ancestor Starcarers would know exactly when it was time to go to care for the stars. That's because they and *only* they would hear the angels singing from the skies above the castle, telling them it was time to go."

Grandad looked back down at the painting in front of them

"Now this painting used to hang above the great fireplace in the castle. The boat in the painting was called a 'galley'. No one really knows where it came from, but we know that it was somewhere far away from the island. And what we also know is that it's very, very old and very, very special. Now there have been many storytellers in our family. They told wonderful stories of what our family did in and with that boat. It's said that Noah himself offered an ancestor of ours to come into his ark to escape the flood, but he had the cheek to tell him *'No thanks' – I've got a boat of my own!*"

Shannon chuckled at this.

"There have been lots of stories of using the boat to defend the castle from enemies, of chasing great whales, of passing mermaids and of sailing to faraway places. But, as you now know, it's the easiest and often the most unwise thing in the world to just imagine that when something's called a 'story' that it isn't true. But sadly that's what grown-ups tend to do. They stopped truly thinking for themselves when they were children and prefer to let other people and the world around them do the 'thinking' for them. But some 'stories' may be very true indeed. I think that you possibly found this out tonight Shannon!" he winked.

"I'll drink to that!" said Angus, holding his cup of tea in the air and clinking it against Grandads, in agreement.

Grandad continued "Now something that our ancestors never really told stories about was that the galley used to sail up here, to care for the stars and moon, *long* before me and my bike did. Only the Starcarers knew about that, of course, but it's absolutely true. As far as we know, until now in our family only one person at a time was chosen as a Starcarer. The reason that they never told stories about that is probably because it was pretty much their secret."

"Wow!" said Shannon. I mean, your bike's amazing enough! But imagine *sailing* up to the stars!"

Grandad nodded and went on "But sadly, things happened and our ancestors had to sell the island and the castle after living there very happily for hundreds of years. The man who bought it didn't care about the island or the people. In fact he tried to starve the people off the island and make them get off it and force them far across the oceans on slave ships to cold, wild places. I'm sorry to say that many who went on those ships died on the way across the sea or soon after getting to those far away lands, which were so strange and hard for them."

Shannon looked sad and shocked "That's terrible Grandad!"

"But do you know what Shannon? Rather than getting on those huge ships, your Great, great, great Grandfather, Neil managed one night to escape in the galley with the box of stardust, the painting and many friends and family and took them across from the island to our home town

53

on the mainland, where we, their children are now. They made new lives here, learnt the language we now speak and built houses for themselves and even the church that we go to today. Now when they built the church, Neil built that safe hiding place for the stardust high up above the altar. You saw it yourself tonight!"

Shannon joked "Oh! The Baldy-Queen, you mean?"

"Yes! That's the one!" grinned Grandad. "You know Shannon, when you look at the boat in this picture, does it look like you've seen it somewhere before?"

Shannon nodded "Yes Grandad, I was thinking that when I first saw the painting tonight".

"Well then, if I tell you that you might have seen it before in the church, in two places?"

Shannon looked down, thinking. Nothing came to mind. Then she remembered being in the church earlier, when she saw Grandad climbing the ladder to get the stardust and the glowing light between the painting above her and the stained glass window. Her eyes widened with excitement as she looked up again.

"Yes Grandad! The galley's in the stained glass window *and* in the background in the painting as you go into the church!"

"You've got it Shannon!" he smiled. "Quite recently they made that picture of the galley on the window, in honour of the island that we came from and the boat that took our family to where we live now. Only Neil knew how special that galley really was. And if you look, you'll even see the castle in the window, behind the galley. And you mentioned the painting as you go in the church, that also shows the galley? Well, we don't really know who Neil asked to do the painting. It could well have been another one done by the angels, or maybe he painted it himself. But if you look closely at it you'll see two different lands, one on each side of the painting. What we do know is that one of the lands shown is where the galley and our ancestors came from, so long ago. On the other side is the island that they sailed to and where they built the castle. So it's a very special picture indeed, just like this one here."

Shannon could listen forever to such amazing things, but she wondered about what happened to the galley and asked Grandad about this.

"Well Shannon, not long after getting to the mainland Neil was told nicely by a visiting angel that the next time that he took the galley up into the skies that it had to stay up here amongst the stars and that its time on the Earth was up. So he took it and left it with the angels. They gave him a beautiful horse instead, which he called Reulach to fly back home on and to use for flying up to keep caring for the stars, with the help of a little stardust, of course! Years later, my Father was given the job of caring for the stars too. One day the angels asked him to leave Reulach with them, as her job was done. The angels themselves flew him back to his home that night, telling him that with the help of some stardust that he could choose whatever he wanted to fly up here. He loved his bike, so he chose that. And I use his bike to this day!"

"But Grandad" said Shannon. "Why does it have wings? I mean, you don't need them to fly up here, do you?" Both Grandad and Leo laughed out loud at this.

"Well Shannon, it's like this. With just stardust the bike flew perfectly, but our Daddy thought that the bike looked a bit boring the way it was. So when he was at a star one day he asked an angel for some spare wings. He got these and fixed them onto the bike. They're not exactly to our taste, but it seemed to make our Daddy happy!" He chuckled, then leaned across the table to Shannon again.

"And Shannon, here's the thing. Only those who are chosen by the angels to look after the stars can move the boat in that picture. That's the way it's always been. Neil could do it when he lived in the castle. And today only Angus, me and now *you* can do it. You've been chosen Shannon! *That's* why I'm *so* happy." Now 'Angus', here, he was the Starcarer before me, but he was told by the angels that he had to take the special honour of caring for the moon instead and that I had to take his job as Starcarer. He checked by showing me the picture here and seeing if the boat moved for me too, without saying anything to me. It did and I was as surprised as you are tonight! But now Shannon, I'm delighted to say that the job seems to be passing to you!"

Shannon just sat, feeling so special and happy. But then something came into her mind. Grandad, 'Tuppence and Uncle Angus knew about the bike and caring for the stars, but who was the other man in the community centre earlier, the one with the hat and glasses on who played the piano? She turned to Grandad and asked him, but he replied "I'm sorry Shannon, but I don't think that it's right for me to tell you that. All I can say is that you do know him and that I think that it's fair to say that if he wants you to know who he is that he'll tell you. Is that all right?" Shannon wasn't too happy with the answer, but nodded her head.

This was the most amazing night of her life! Her head eventually turned as Angus tossed a golf-ball into the air and caught it beside her. "Right!" he said "After all that, I think we'd best drink up. We've got a round of moongolf to play, you know!

Chapter 7- Moongolf

Shannon gulped down her sugarelly and walked into the hall, where Grandad and Angus struggled to get two golf bags from a cupboard. "Oh come on!" she laughed. "You can't be *serious*? Golf on the moon!" Grandad and Angus just grinned, throwing the golf bags over their shoulders. The clubs in their bags clattered as they opened the door to the wide sparkling black skies of space in front of them. "Are you coming then Shannon?" they asked.

She followed on. She'd never so much as held a golf-club before, let alone dreamt of playing the game on the moon! They walked down the path through the flowering garden and out onto the grey, dusty moon surface.

"This is crazy!" laughed Shannon! "Where do you start from...and where do you hit to?"

Angus kept walking ahead and pointed in front of them.

"Over there" he said, pointing to a rock.

As they got to it, Shannon noticed that the rock had a neat '1' painted on it. There was a bit of flat, firm, grey ground nearby and Grandad pointed out a red flag away in the distance. Angus and Grandad took off their golf bags and started to get a ball and club ready.

"I've never played before though – so I'll just watch." said Shannon.

Angus turned to her, his hands rummaging around in his golfbag

"Oh, it's never too late to start and you'll have plenty of chances to have a shot at hitting the ball today, Shannon. But for now, could you do us a favour and do the 'Gravity Control' for us?"

As he said this, he handed Shannon a small, carved wooden box, with a tiny lever sticking out of the top of it. She looked down at it, wondering what on earth it was! "Emmm…Uncle Angus. Sorry, but what do I do with this?" Grandad and Angus grinned to each other, as Grandad took a swig from a small bottle that he took from his bag "I never thought you'd ask, Shannon! Now in all honesty, golf's a game that only a very few people can ever truly play really well. The only person I *ever* knew to play golf incredibly well was your Grandad's brother, Leo!" Grandad spluttered out his drink, almost choking in his laughter. "Oh, you *think* so 'Angus!" he said "Perhaps he wasn't *that* good!"

Angus carried on "Anyway Shannon, for the rest of us, we sometimes need a little 'help' to make our game a wee bit better. So that's what the Gravitor in your hand is for." Shannon looked down at the wooden box, then back up to Angus "Gravitor'?" she asked, puzzled. "Uh-huh!" said Angus, placing the ball on the flat piece of ground in front of him and lining up his golf-club to give it a good whack towards the flag. As he stood there waiting to swing, he told Shannon what to do "Now Shannon, when we hit the ball, we *might* ask you to move the wee stick on the Gravitor either backwards or forwards, all right?"

"All right" she nodded.

With that he looked down towards the flag and back to the ball, saying "Only move it if I say so please Shannon". His club swung backwards, then whacked the ball and watched it fly through the starry sky towards the flag. Shannon waited quietly to hear if he asked for the stick to be moved, but he said "That's fine Shannon – no need for the Gravitor for *that* shot!" He stepped back and her Grandad placed his ball on the ground, shaking his head and grinning saying quietly to himself "You jammy so-and-so Angus!" He spoke louder to Shannon. "All right Shannon – the same for me please. Move the stick on the Gravitor only if

I ask you to please" Shannon nodded. He lined up his club, looked at the flag in the distance and back at the ball, his club swung back and then quickly down. "*Whack!*" the ball flew forwards, but almost hitting the ground.

"*Now!*" screamed Grandad "...move the lever backwards Shannon!" Shannon flicked the tiny lever and then got the shock of her life! Suddenly she felt incredibly light. She, Grandad, Angus and their golf bags started to float slightly off the ground! "Oh my *goodness*, Grandad!" she shouted in fright. But Grandad and Angus kept looking forward towards the ball, which was still flying forwards, but higher from the ground now. Grandad watched as the ball got closer to the flag, his hand pointing behind him towards Shannon "All right Shannon...hold it....hold it.......lever forward....*now!*" shouted Grandad. Shannon did as he said and suddenly they fell the few centimetres back down to the ground – and so did the golf-ball in the distance. She was shaking...and *so* happy to be back down. "Woooo...hooo!" shouted Grandad! "You *did* it Shannon! The ball's almost in the hole!" he laughed. "And you call *me* jammy!" said Angus. He pointed towards the Earth. "Och Jimmy! You know fine that if you hit that shot down there that it would have only gone about 50 feet!" Grandad just laughed as he put his club back into the bag and started to walk away towards his ball, saying "You made the rules up here Angus. And your Gravitor's a *great* invention! Don't drop it Shannon" Grandad chuckled. Angus winked at Shannon and they followed on.

It was quite the most amazing experience. Grandad and Angus showed Shannon how to hit the ball, but what *fun* they had using the Gravitor to make shots better - or worse sometimes, to tease each other! They'd put on the Gravitor and take *huge*, floating leaps across the ground. Shannon learnt to flip over slowly in mid-air when it was on! The views were simply amazing. Twinkling starry skies all around them and the occasional shooting star whooshing by. As they played, Shannon noticed the bright daytime light slowly edge around the earth in the distance and get closer to lighting up her town. They went back to the house and had a cheerful chat over a cup of tea, before Grandad looked out towards the Earth, saying that it was time to go.

As Grandad was outside getting the bike ready, Angus gave Shannon a hug. He looked her in the eyes and said
"Shannon, can you guess why I've got the Gravitor, why I'd want to be able to make things either float or stay down up here?"
"Emmm... to make golf better fun Uncle Angus?"
" Well, that's indeed a nice 'effect' of the Gravitor Shannon!" he laughed
"But we really have it because we want to protect and care for the moon. Shannon, people have always looked up at the moon from Earth and wished that they could come up here; wondered what the moon was really like. I'm sure that you've done the same yourself. But recently it looks more and more like people might at last be able to build a rocket to take them up here. Now if they came up here and found that it was fine to live on, they'd tell the people on earth and more and more people would come. Many people wouldn't care for the moon and it's very likely that they'd ruin it."
Shannon looked worried.
"That's why the angels and I thought of the 'Gravitor' Shannon! If and when someone comes up here, all we have to do is turn it on, they'll see that the moon's too hard to stay on because everything floats - and they'll hopefully go away!"
Shannon smiled "That's a *great* idea Uncle Angus!"

He went to the mantelpiece above the fire and took down a small ornament of a brown horse. "Here you go Shannon – a wee souvenir of your first visit here!" She thanked him and carefully put the ornament in her pocket, asking "Did you say *'first'*, Uncle Angus? So I can come back, then?"

"Of *course* you can Shannon! Come up whenever your Grandad comes up, he'll know when it's best to." Angus looked out the window and saw that Grandad was ready to go, puffing away on his pipe. They went out to the bike and Shannon got into the box-trailer. As she got in she heard a 'clunk' of bottles. She looked down around her feet and saw three bottles of sugarelly. "Now how on earth did *they* get in there?" winked Uncle Angus. "Thanks Uncle!" smiled Shannon. Grandad and Shannon put on their goggles and Grandad chucked a small handful of stardust into the air above them. "See you later!" shouted Grandad, as Angus waved. The wings glowed and suddenly they were off again, gliding down towards the Earth. Shannon looked behind them and saw the moon slowly get smaller and smaller. In just a few minutes they arrived back at the darkness of the park at the museum, where Tuppence was waiting. He was shocked to see Shannon and asked Grandad how she managed to be up at the stars. But Grandad just said he'd tell him later and asked him to hurry to help get the bike into the museum shed before anyone saw them. In the bike went and they shut the doors behind them. Once inside, Grandad quickly explained it all to Tuppence, about how Shannon saw them earlier at the church and sneaked into the box trailer. Tuppence looked so disappointed and worried, but once Grandad explained that she had moved the galley-boat in the picture, his eyes lit up and he hugged Shannon with joy. They left the museum together, walked past the statue of the Doctor and down the tree-edged road towards the Police Station at the bottom. Along the road and quietly into the church they went and

'Tuppence held the ladder again as Grandad climbed up and gently placed the stardust tin safely back in its resting place. As he did this, Shannon gasped as the golden beam of light shone again from the galley boat in the picture at the entrance of the church, across to the other picture of the galley in the stained glass window and then all the way down the church and above her to the tin. She smiled to herself – now she *knew* why this happened.

They went back out onto the gravel of the churchyard, quietly closing the door behind them. Tuppence wished them goodnight at the gate and walked off through the dark streets towards his own house. She liked visiting his house. His garden walls were decorated with millions of pieces of coloured glass and whisky bottle tops he'd fixed into it. Shannon and Grandad walked the other way and were soon close to his house, Maybank. He stopped walking and handed Shannon a tiny, flowery, metal box with golden edges and said
"Shannon, tomorrow this might all seem like a dream to you. Keep this tin somewhere *very* safe - it has stardust inside. It's only because you're now a Starcarer that I can give you this. When you're safely on your own open it up and look inside to remind you that it's all true. And please Shannon, *never* tell anyone about all this. Nobody will believe you and they'll only laugh at you if you tell them. And if they do believe you, the stars could end up ruined, with everyone wanting to visit."
"All right Grandad, I'll try my best." They walked on and were soon outside Grandad's house. No lights on – a good sign, as Granny surely would have waited up all night for Shannon to come back if she'd found that she'd sneaked out. They crept in as quietly as they could. There was no sign of Granny, so Shannon was happy that it looked like she wouldn't

be in trouble. "Goodnight. God-bless my wee Starcarer!" whispered Grandad in the hallway, kissing her on the forehead. "Away you go up and try to get some sleep." He climbed the stairs quietly to his room. Shannon crept slowly up to her room straight afterwards. There she found the pile of pillows and blankets still in her bed, just as she'd left them. 'Thank Goodness!' she thought. She opened the tiny flowery box and had a last look for tonight inside at the glowing stardust and then hid it under her wardrobe. Her mind whizzed with amazing thoughts. *What* a night! Already she could hardly believe it all. But she still had school tomorrow. She looked at the hands on her clock – 3am! She dozed off to sleep....still smiling!

Chapter 8 – Down to Earth

'Clang-alang-alang-alang-alang-alang-alang-alang-alang..!' Shannon's
hand slapped off the alarm-clock. She was absolutely exhausted and
soon dozed off again. The next thing she knew, Granny was racing about
her room like a cheery tornado

"Come on Sleepy-bones! My, you're awfully snoozy today my girl! Did
your alarm clock not go off? Let's get you up for school then! Bright eyed
and bushy tailed! Your breakfast's waiting for you."

Granny was always so bright and cheery in the morning! Shannon never
knew how she managed it! She took down a sheet of black paper from
the window and sunlight streamed in, hurting Shannon's eyes with its
brightness. "Come on now Shannon, wakey wakey!" said Granny, as she
raced out of the room.

Shannon struggled up and tried to look out the window. It was covered in
fantastic swirling frosty patterns. She rubbed the window with a finger to
see outside. The back garden was covered in sparkling frost. Shannon
hated going to the outside toilet shed first thing – especially when it was
freezing! She went down the stairs in her nightgown, wiping the sleep
from her eyes as she yawned and stepped out into the frosty morning in
the back garden. She shivered as she opened the wooden door of the
toilet, partly with the cold and partly because she was checking for
spiders. They always seemed to *love* outside toilets, for some odd
reason. After a minute or so on that freezing toilet, Shannon's sleepiness
had *absolutely* disappeared and suddenly she remembered absolutely
everything that happened the night before too. She climbed the stairs
again and got washed and dressed, then came back downstairs

and pushed open the door of the kitchen. As usual, Granny was stood at the cooker, stirring some porage. Grandad was sat at the table, reading his newspaper - a teapot, rack of toast, butter and marmalade on the middle of the table in front of him.

Grandad put his paper down and smiled through his glasses at Shannon as Granny cheerily announced "Good morning Sleepy-bones! You made it then!"

"'Morning Granny, morning Grandad." she replied, as she pulled her chair out and sat down. It was a bit strange that morning, because Grandad and Shannon knew a secret about the stars and moon that Granny didn't know. It almost seemed unfair, but Shannon remembered what Grandad told her about not telling anyone about it. The last thing that Shannon wanted for Granny to think was that she was being foolish, or for Granny to maybe get angry with Grandad for "telling her stories" again!

Granny poured some porage into a bowl for her. It's such a great thing for warming up your tummy before you walk through the cold air to school! As usual, Granny opened a tin of golden syrup as a topping for the porridge, dipped in a spoon and spun it slowly it over the plate to stop it dripping. Shannon found herself staring at the dripping syrup and was immediately thought of the goldenness of the stars the night before. She saw Grandad's face ahead, past the syrup. He winked and smiled, like he knew exactly what she was thinking.

"Quite a frosty morning Shannon" said Granny. This porage will keep you warm for the walk to school.

"Emm…yes Granny!" she replied.

Granny sat down next to her "What's the matter my girl? You're very sleepy this morning. It's like your hardly here! Did you have a problem sleeping last night then?" She suddenly looked concerned "Everything all right, my dear?"

Shannon nodded "Yes Granny – I'm fine. I just didn't get a lot of sleep last night, I kept waking up with strange dreams."

Granny took the woollen tea-cosy off of the teapot and started to pour. "Och well, eat up Shannon – and it's an early night for you tonight then, so you can catch up on sleep."

Shannon nodded and ate up her warming, sweet porridge and a couple of slices of marmalade covered, buttery toast, then grabbed her coat, scarf and schoolbag from the hall.

She rushed upstairs to her room and got the tiny tin of stardust from under her wardrobe – she just *had* to see it again, before she went out! She opened it and her eyes and face lit up as the golden glow glittered inside. She poked the very end of a fingertip gently into it and stared at the twinkling spot on her finger. There was simply no colour like this anywhere else but up there. She hid her glowing finger in her pocket and rushed down the stairs and poked her head back into the kitchen to say goodbye to Granny and Grandad. Granny gave her a big, warm hug, saying

"Have a great day my dear. You work hard now and make your Dad proud of you for when he sees you again!"

Grandad hugged her straight after and said

"I'm pretty sure that her Dad's very proud of her already Granny. Go on Shannon, off to school and make sure you're the *Star*-pupil!" he winked.

Shannon giggled at this "No problem Grandad…'bye."

Shannon smiled through most of Mrs Grant's lesson that morning. Louisa could see she was very happy, but of course, Shannon couldn't tell her why. They were doing more on their project about space. The pictures on the walls and paper stars hanging from the lights were very good, but not anything like as good as the real thing. It meant *so* much more to Shannon now. At one time Mrs Grant even said that it seemed impossible to think that one day people might go to the moon! Shannon couldn't help but giggle to herself, which she tried (badly!) to disguise as a cough. Mrs Grant looked over at her - and she didn't exactly look too happy. She was about to give her a telling off when suddenly a strange, loud howl screamed out. "Right class!" shouted Mrs Grant through the noise. "That's the Air-raid practice alarm! Grab your gasmask boxes and line up at the door in an orderly fashion!"

'Great!' Thought everyone in the class. Excitement! Although it did seem very strange to all of them. After all, they lived in the middle of nowhere, hundreds of miles from a big city. Who in their right minds would bother to fly a plane up here and bomb anything, unless they had something against sheep and tractors? Still, they loved the fun of practising! And this was the first chance to wear their new 'Mickey Mouse' gasmasks that Mr Sandcroft, the Warden had taken round for everyone at the school last month. Like their last gasmasks, they still had a horrible rubber smell, but they were so much more fun. They had two big, round eye bits and even had whiskers...and Mickey Mouse ears. They put on their masks and lined up. Everyone tried not to giggle as they looked around at each other in those mousey masks! Mrs Grant went to the front of the line and led them out to the playground. As they walked behind, everyone brought their hands together up close to their chins and scurried along, pretending to be mice! If Mrs Grant had seen them they'd be in trouble, but it was too much fun to miss. Louisa and Shannon were in tears of laughter. They stood grinning in their line in the playground, trying to

control their giggles. Then the next class stood up next to them. Shannon looked sideways and her smiling suddenly stopped when she saw that Veronica was standing in the next line *right* beside her. Her year didn't get the funny looking mousey gasmasks. Instead they had the 'ordinary' big ones. Veronica turned sideways to give a nasty look at Shannon. With that mask on, Veronica looked frightening, like an evil crow, staring at her. Shannon was certainly frightened of her and quickly turned her head towards the front. All the pupils went quiet as their names were called out by the class teachers. The tall figure of the school Headmaster, Mr Morran walked carefully forward to face the pupils, his wife holding his arm. He stood tall in his usual, smart pin-stripe suit. He was definitely the nicest teacher that they had and Shannon loved the class music sessions with him. He must have known a million songs! There was something special about him though. He had been blind since he was born. Even a little girl like Shannon knew that his being blind must have been what gave him such a love of music. He started to tell the school how well everyone had done in getting out quickly and into line and then asked the teachers to take everyone back inside. He was such a nice man that Shannon almost forgot that Veronica was beside her.

But *then* she remembered *very* well! She felt her gasmask being pulled forward off her face by Veronica, who then let it ping back, sore against Shannon's nose and mouth. She started to cry at the pain. She heard Veronica giggling, but then heard Louisa shouting *"Right!"* and pushing into the much bigger Veronica, knocking her back onto the playground floor. Everyone around moved back and an angry Mrs Grant came running across from the front. She grabbed Veronica and Louisa from the ground and shouted for them to put their gas-masks back in their boxes in the classroom and then to get straight to Mr Morran's room – *"Now"*! Shannon came out of line and tried to tell the red-faced Mrs Grant that it wasn't Louisa's fault, but Mrs Grant was in no mood to have anyone else disturb today. "You too Shannon McNeil! Put your gasmask away and then get yourself *straight* to Mr Morran's room as well!" The three girls stood quietly outside the office. Even Veronica was scared about getting in trouble with a teacher. It was always double trouble, because when you got home, you were also in trouble with your parents too!

Veronica was taken in first. Shannon and Louisa tried to listen carefully at what was being said, or shouted, behind Mr Morran's big, dark, wooden door. Shannon whispered across to Louisa "Thanks for sticking up for me Louisa". Louisa smiled back "No problem Shannon – that's what friends are for. And anyway, it was worth it to see that horrible Veronica flopping about on the playground floor like a landed fish!" They quietly giggled to each other about that. But then stopped, scared again, as the door clicked open. Veronica walked out, her eyes puffed up with tears. Mr Morran's voice boomed out from the office inside "Louisa McHardy....in you come!" She quietly walked past Shannon into the office, the girls touching each other's hands for luck as she walked in, before that big, dark door closed behind her.

Shannon listened as hard as she could, but couldn't make out what was being said. Her heart thumped in her chest, wondering what trouble she'd be in. She rubbed her nose and mouth, still red and sore from the bang of the gasmask. She was scared at going into the office, but also so angry at Veronica. A few minutes later she jumped slightly as that big door clicked and creaked opened again. Louisa walked out, head down and obviously upset. She tapped Shannon's hand on the way past again and went back to the class. "Shannon McNeil...in you come." boomed out Mr Morran's voice again. She walked in and stood in front of Mr Morran's desk and saw Mrs Morran sitting at another desk in the next room behind him.

"Sit down Shannon" he said. She was surprised that he didn't sound very angry. "Now Shannon, tell me what happened out there, then."

"Well, Veronica pulled my gasmask forwards off my face and let it ping back and it really hurt! She did it for no reason at all and my lip's bleeding too, look!" she pointed to her lip and then she instantly felt terrible, as she'd asked a blind-man to look. "No, Mr Morran, I'm sorry…I didn't mean….!"

"Don't worry Shannon" he smiled "I know what you meant. And Louisa McHardy…..?"

"Oh" said Shannon, she's my best pal and I suppose that she just got annoyed at Veronica being so nasty and decided to push her for being nasty to me."

Mr Morran sat back in his chair, seeming quite content with what Shannon said "That's exactly what Louisa told me happened Shannon. And that's what I heard happening too. Don't worry, you're not in trouble now. Louisa's been given a punishment exercise to do, because she shouldn't have pushed someone. And I can assure you that Veronica will have a *lot* of homework to do for the next two weeks!" He took a small piece of paper from a tray on top of the desk, signed it and held it out to Shannon. "Take this note with you and give it to Mrs Grant, Shannon. But first go to the Nurses Station and make sure that your lip's all right." "Yes, Mr Morran, thank you Mr Morran". As Shannon took the piece of paper from Mr Morran's hand she saw his face change, like he'd suddenly got a shock. "Oh my Goodness…!" he whispered. Shannon wondered what was wrong "Are you all right, Mr Morran?" His wife had heard Shannon speaking and she stood up, concerned as he sat down. "I'm all right, thank you." He turned to his wife. "My dear, would you do me a favour and get me a cup of tea? I'm just feeling a bit dry. I'll be fine." he assured Mrs Morran as she left the room. Shannon didn't know what to do, but she was worried that Mr Morran wasn't feeling too well.

But he sat back in his chair and just grinned widely "Shannon McNeil – I'll bet your Grandad's proud!" She was confused. "What do you mean Mr Morran?"

"Shannon, what have you got on the pointing finger on your left hand? Something special, perhaps?" Shannon looked down and saw the remaining twinkle of some stardust on her finger from the morning. She panicked. How could he know? And *what* did he know?" "Emmm, I've got some, ehhh.....paint!"

Mr Morran smiled widely "Oh, but I've never known paint to be such a wonderful colour before Shannon!"

"But Mr Morran, excuse me saying this but....you're blind! How could you see a colour?" He sat forward, leaning across the desk. "Now Shannon, just because these eyes have never worked, it doesn't mean that I can't *see* what's true, what's good, does it? Now Shannon that's stardust on your finger, isn't it? I could feel the goodness of it when you took the piece of paper."

Shannon got really worried.

"Don't panic Shannon. I know that if you've got that on you and it's feeling so true that it can only be that you're a Starcarer – just like your Grandad! I'm absolutely delighted for you. Well done!"

Shannon gasped "Yes, Mr Morran! I am. But how did you know?"

"You mean that your Grandad never told you? About your UncleTuppence and me?"

"Well, I know that Uncle Tuppence and Grandad know all about this, but I didn't know that you did too!" Shannon suddenly recognised a hat hanging up in the corner of the room. "Wait a minute Mr Morran. The hat, the piano - *you're* the third man that I saw in the community centre with Grandad and Uncle Tuppence, aren't you?" gasped Shannon Mr Morran laughed, walked his way round the desk and stuck his hand out to shake hers. "It seems like I am! Congratulations Shannon. What a truly *wonderful* thing to be a Starcarer. Don't worry, the secret's *very* safe between us all!"

The door creaked open again and Mrs Morran appeared with the cup of tea and placed it on Mr Morran's desk. "Well Shannon, you head back to class now – we'll talk again some other time." Mrs Morran cheerily said to him "Well, you're looking a lot better now!" as Shannon left the room. She walked back into her class with a huge grin on her face and sat down next to Louisa, slapping her hand in friendship. Louisa stared at her. How could she be smiling after getting told off?

The smile never left Shannon's face all day. The bell went and she soon cheered Louisa up with a few funny voices – so they left the school together smiling. They walked down to the end of the road and turned round the corner. There behind a wall was Veronica with some of her nasty pals! Without saying anything she pulled Louisa's hair and pushed her back hard on the road, kicking her on the leg as she fell. Shannon ran at Veronica to defend Louisa, but Veronica and her pals were just too big. Shannon ended up sore on the ground too. Veronica and her pals walked away, laughing. Shannon and Louisa helped each other up. Louisa was crying and shouted at Veronica, who just laughed. Shannon and Louisa helped each other along the road until they got to the place where the roads split, hugged each other and went to their homes. Shannon crept slowly into her Mum's house and got herself washed up, in case Mum saw that she'd been hurt. She didn't want to upset her. All that evening and later as she lay in her bed Shannon had happy thoughts about Mr Morran and how amazing it was that he was involved with the stars. She took one of the window covering sheets off and stared up at the night sky. They meant *so* much to her now. She was also a bit annoyed at herself for not believing in them before - that she had to actually go up and see and be right beside them with Grandad to know this. But also she had angry thoughts about that horrible Veronica and how bad she was to Louisa and herself. Something *must* be done about her! She slowly dozed off to sleep thinking about all of these things.

Chapter 9 – A Message

Since her husband, Johnny had to go away to war, Mum had a new 'routine' that she stuck to every night. As the alarm clock's hand reached 10 o'clock, she put down her book, kissed his photograph goodnight and clicked off the bedside lamp. She and Daddy had agreed to think of each other every night at that time, to know that they were with each other. If possible, to look up at the moon at that time; knowing that they were both looking at the same thing. He had thought of it. She remembered how embarrassed he was to tell her about this idea, in case she thought it was stupid. But now, she was so glad that he had asked her to. So many things around the room and around the house reminded her of him, almost like he'd never gone at all; and could walk back in at any minute. The bed seemed so big without him there. She could have just spread out in the middle, but always still slept on her side of the bed leaving his side for him. She didn't listen to the news – it only made her worry. As she often did, she got angry about how stupid this whole war was .That all she really cared about was getting him back to her. And she knew that every wife and Mother all around this silly war felt the same, no matter what country they were from. And as usual, she lay there in the dark, closed her eyes and imagined herself leaving her body and flying to him. She almost believed that if she did this, part of her would really be with him, wherever he was. She imagined flying out of the house along the dark streets, down the High Street, towards and over the harbour and out to sea, turning towards and over the dark mountains, across the glittering dark water of the channel, over foreign fields until she came to a waiting, quiet battleground. She pictured looking down at soldiers resting all around the muddy field in the silent night. With her eyes closed she tried so hard to picture slowly coming down from the sky and seeing him sitting there, finding some time to rest. She pictured herself gently coming down right next to him, sitting by him, hugging him, kissing him - and telling him just how much she loved him. Sometimes this made her cry, sometimes feel so warm, but always, feel so very close to him. This was their personal time together. Tonight, as always, she said her prayers for him, for his daughter, Shannon and for all people caught up in this crazy war. She reached out again for his photo and kissed it in the dark and slowly drifted off to sleep. She dreamt about her Johnny that night, of him hugging her on the beach, just down the road. They laughed amongst the sand dunes, played games with Shannon. But he suddenly turned her so quickly to him in the sea breeze with a serious look in his eyes and said: *"Don't be afraid Evelyn. And always know that I love you and Shannon more than I can possibly tell you; and that I'll always be with you."* He was so serious, so urgent after the laughing that Mum woke and sat up in the dark bedroom, worrying, knowing that something was wrong....and there he was...Johnny! He stood there at the foot of their bed, in his kilted uniform and kilt cover on. The moonlight shone on the side of his face. She was amazed, confused...was she still dreaming? She saw his wonderful smile. It seemed he moved so slowly, blowing her a kiss. This can't be a dream. "Johhny?" she heard herself whispering. He stared at her so lovingly, never said a word and just shook his head sadly, slowly turned round and disappeared into the darkness. She sat up, chilled, amazed. Her shaking hand reached for the water by her bed and she drank. She wasn't dreaming! Her eyes stared so hard into the darkness of the wall to try to see him. But she knew.....he was gone...! Her Johnny had come to tell her he'd been killed! She heard herself scream and burst into tears. The next thing she knew was the flash of the light going on and just seeing that wall. Her Shannon's startled face appeared round the door. She had heard the scream. Fear blanketed her face. Mum spent a few seconds just staring at Shannon's face, realising her daughter's Father was dead. Then a wave of realisation washed over her, telling her that deep she had to be strong for her girl. She reached open her arms "Come on here Shannon, it's all right...Mummy just had a bad dream!" Shannon bounced onto the bed, still upset seeing Mum's teary face and hugged her. "There, there Shannon". Shannon asked her what the dream was about and tried to reassure her. Mum just kept hugging her wee girl tightly, trying hard not to let any crying out – trying to be strong.

CHAPTER 10 – Memories And Golden Wings

It was the next morning, Saturday. Shannon went down the stairs and was surprised to find Mum hunched over in her armchair, listening to the news on the radio with her ear almost touching it. "Morning Mum!" said Shannon. Mum jumped with fright and turned. She looked nervous and tired. "*Sshhhhhhh*!" she said and quickly turned her head to listen close to the radio again. Shannon was a bit shocked. She'd hardly ever really seen Mum in a mood like this before. On the radio they were talking about the war. Mum had never listened to that. She said that it was better not to know what's happening. Shannon quietly wandered through to the kitchen and spread some bread and jam for breakfast. She smiled as she spread the juicy jelly on the thick bread, remembering two nights ago, when she was up amongst the stars and moon. But then she also remembered that Mum must have had a terrible nightmare last night. She hated to see Mum upset. She pushed the door open a tiny bit and peeked through to the sitting room to see her. She still had her ear up to the radio, listening. Shannon poured a glass of milk and made Mum some bread and jam and took it through to her. As she walked across the room with the plate and glass in her hand Mum never even moved. "Here's a jammy piece and some milk for you Mum." she said, placing them on the table. Mum never even looked, but mumbled a quick "Yes…thanks Shannon" like Shannon had disturbed her.

Shannon was off to Grandad's this morning to go with him on his bike to help him with some painting jobs. It was now time to go. "I'd best be off to Grandad's Mum." She waited for Mum to say something, or at least to turn round – but she didn't. She went over and stood beside Mum, who still stared at the radio. Shannon gently put her arm over Mum's shoulder and snuggled against her. "What's the matter Mum? Are you missing Daddy?" she felt Mum shake and her head look up to the ceiling. "It's alright Mum, Daddy's probably just playing football with his friends over in France right now. And he told us he'd be home for Christmas". Mum's arm jerked up and she wiped her eyes with her hand. Shannon walked round to the fireplace in front of Mum and saw her eyes red with tears and her nose all sniffly. "Mum, what's the matter?" asked Shannon again, feeling herself starting to cry at the sight of Mum's tears. Mum sniffled and put a fake smile on her face.

"Oh, nothing Shannon. Don't worry about me. I'm not crying about anything really. You run along to Grandad's. On you go Shannon, I'll be fine!" Shannon knew that she wasn't crying for nothing, but she didn't know what was upsetting her. She also knew that sometimes it's best not to ask. She slowly left the room, feeling bad about Mum's tears

"I'll see you later Mum. I love you!"

"I love you too Shannon. Be good for Grandad. And I've left some liquorice out on the coat-stand for you to make some sugarelly at Grandad's for yourself! Be good!"

Shannon walked slowly to Grandad's with her head down. She felt a lump in her throat grow as she thought of Mum crying. *Is there anything worse than seeing your Mother cry?* she thought. She didn't even run along the tops of the walls today. Instead she just ambled slowly along until she eventually walked through Grandad's front door.

Grandad and Granny noticed that she was a bit sad looking and asked why. Shannon explained that Mum was crying this morning and Granny gave her a big hug and said not to worry and that she'd go round to Mum's and see how she was later and sort things out. "*Right* my little Cowgirly! Are you ready to come out painting with your old Grandad today then, eh?" shouted Grandad, rubbing his hands together and grinning widely. Shannon smiled for the first time that day. He grabbed his cap and slung on his jacket, saying "Come on then, let's mosey downtown then, these windowsills won't paint themselves you know!" He kissed Granny, saying "See you later Dear! Always with you." Shannon then hugged her and followed out behind Grandad, as Granny said behind her "Go on then, you have fun and don't worry about Mummy, she'll be fine! And take good care of your Grandad for me too Shannon. He might look like a responsible old man, but he's got the mind and mischief of a six year old boy!" she winked. "Oh, you'd have been bored of me loooong ago if that wasn't true, my dear!" laughed Grandad.

Shannon felt a lot better now as she walked hand in hand down the road to Grandad's painting workshop. As they walked, she could talk about nothing else but their trip to the stars two nights ago. Grandad loved that it was so special to her, but kept having to ask her to talk quieter in case someone over-heard. They got to Grandad's wooden workshop and opened up. It wasn't the healthiest of places to breathe in, but Shannon *loved* the smells in there - a mixture of paint and pipe-smoke, which always reminded her of Grandad. She was surprised to see that the bike was in Grandad's workshop waiting for them and was just looking like a normal bike, with no wings again. Grandad explained that Tuppence had taken the wings off of the bike and brought it round from the museum for him this morning. "Right!" He said. "We've two jobs to do today my lady. Firstly we've got some windows to do for the Marine Hotel and then we're off out the road to RAF Brackla for a great job – painting an aeroplane!"

Shannon was so excited about this and placed some tins of paint, a step-ladder, brushes and other painter's things into the wooden trailer until it was almost full.

Grandad pushed the bike outside onto the pavement followed by Shannon, but then looked across the road towards the tall war-memorial, surrounded by lots of poppy-wreaths. He leant the bike against his workshop wall.

"Shannon, would you mind if I showed you something before we head off?" he said, still staring across the road.

"Of course not Grandad!"

"Hold on here a second" he said, as he dashed back into the workshop and came out again with a small picture frame by his side. He took her hand and led her across the road to the memorial. As they crunched across the gravel, its tall, sandstone column towered above them. Grandad stood her near the front of it. "You know what this memorial's for, don't you Shannon?" She did, as she had got a project on it at school recently and knew it was a memorial to men killed in wars. "Well, have you ever stopped to look at it at all?"

"Not really Grandad."

"Well" he smiled "I think that you should have a good look at the names all around it and see if you recognise any of them. I'll have a quick puff on my pipe on the bench over there and if you find the names of two people on here that you know, I'll buy you a bottle of lemonade!" He went to the bench and was soon sitting surrounded by a cloud of pipe-smoke, watching the world go by. There were so many names on the memorial. Shannon's eyes looked up and down, side to side, looking for any names she might recognise. Nothing on the front bit. She moved round until she thought that she'd never see any familiar names, until she ended up right round at the front again.

"It's no use Grandad. I can't find any name I recognise!" Grandad grinned, still puffing.

"Shannon, try the back panel again." She did and as her eyes moved down they suddenly lit up.

"McNeil!" she said! "Two of them! Alexander and John. Are they our family?" she asked. Grandad stood up and came across to Shannon as they both looked at the names.

"They're my brothers Shannon. I have five brothers and we all went to war, just like our Dad. Only four of us came back though."

"Oh…I'm sorry Grandad!"

"Och, don't be!" he said, cheerily "Trust me, they're a lot happier where they are than we are down here! It was our poor Mum who really suffered, not us. She was far too wise to think that there was anything sensible about swapping bullets or torpedoes with someone we don't know, just because someone else told us to. She didn't bring us up to be soldiers. She just wanted us to be happy and settle down. When we all joined the Army and Marines we were all just young lads, really. To be honest, we just joined to get a nice uniform, a job and to try and be heroes!" he laughed. "The strange thing is that we all just found out that the other young lads we were 'fighting' were just the same as us! All they wanted was to be with their families and to enjoy life! They had nothing against us, really! A bit of a silly thing, war, eh?" Shannon looked up at him and nodded. He held up the picture frame in his hand and showed it to Shannon "And this framed newspaper article is all about your family." Shannon took the frame and looked at the newspaper clipping. It said 'Fighting Father of Six Fighting Sons.' In the middle of the clipping was a picture of Great-Granny and Great-Grandad sitting down in the front room at their home in Maybank. Down each side were three face pictures of Grandad and his brothers in uniform. Shannon pointed at a young man's face with a smart looking navy hat on!

"Wow! Is that you Grandad?" "Yep!" he laughed! "Wasn't I a handsome young devil!" He pointed out the others "That's John, Leo, Me, Frank, Willie and Alexander, but we called him Sandy. So the Johnny and Alexander on this memorial here are my brothers, the ones that never came back". Shannon turned to the memorial again and gently touched the names, then turned back to Grandad.

"I've heard you mention Leo a lot, Grandad!" Grandad grinned widely again.

"Oh yes! Leo! Well, I love all of my brothers, but maybe Leo and me used to have the best laughs together. He passed on a few years ago. You were at his funeral, but you were only a baby at the time." Shannon looked sad again.

"I'm sorry Grandad!" Grandad grabbed her shoulders, still smiling.

"As I say, never be Shannon. He's far happier where he is now than we are down here, *believe* me! All right Shannon, let's get back to this bike and get these jobs done".

As Shannon took Grandad's hand to walk back across to the bike, she noticed him drop the picture frame on the gravel. He suddenly stopped and held onto his chest with his hand. He looked to be very sore indeed and out of breath. Shannon didn't know that he'd been having problems with his heart for a while now.

"Grandad! Are you all right?" He still held onto his chest and sat down on the gravel for a few seconds before answering

"I'll be fine Shannon. Don't worry." He sat down for a couple more minutes and seemed to be better. "Well, well" he joked. "I *knew* that I shouldn't have eaten a whole horse for breakfast this morning!" Shannon smiled, but was still concerned inside for Grandad. She knew that he was old and not too well recently. He got on his bike and Shannon climbed up and sat across its bar.

They pedalled on down through the town and right down the road until they were by the big, pointy bandstand, which was near to a steep, grassy hill, called Bunker's Brae. Grandad stopped the bike and nodded his head in that direction. "You see Bunker's Brae there Shannon?" "Yes Grandad" said Shannon. "It's excellent for sledging in the winter. It's *so* steep!" Grandad laughed.

"Oh, steep it *is*! Well Shannon, you were asking me before about Uncle Leo? Well I'll tell you something about him and that hill. Years ago he was joking with a pal of his, called William by telling him that if he just made some wooden and paper wings that that he could fly right off that steep hill. The poor man believed him and he spent two months making some wings! Leo didn't want to tell him that he was joking, in case he felt silly for believing him. But he also didn't want the poor man to get hurt! So the day came that they stood at the top of the steep hill, with some homemade wings, made of paper and wood strapped to William's back, ready to jump off. Thankfully it was only him and Leo that were there, otherwise William would have *really* got laughed at. Leo didn't want him to get hurt, so he sneaked a tiny touch of stardust onto the wings, when he wasn't looking. Well the man ran forward and got the shock of his life as he took off into the sky for about twenty seconds or so, until the stardust wore off and he landed with a clunk on the grass below!"

Shannon laughed out loud at this. "*Really* Grandad?"

"Yes and you know the worst thing? The poor man believed that his wings could really make him fly, but Leo couldn't just keep putting stardust on his wings, or people would find out about it. So for the next few years the poor man kept throwing himself off the top of the Bunkers Brae, trying to fly again but always landing in a crumpled heap at the bottom of the hill!"

"Awww!" said Shannon, trying not to laugh.

"Oh, you're right Shannon. It was a shame, but pretty funny at the same time!" he laughed. "He was a happy man though, no matter how people laughed at his attempts to fly, he kept trying and he never gave up. I think that man deserves his name on a monument on that hill for his determination!"

They cycled on and got to the Marine Hotel and Shannon helped out to paint some windowsills and clean some brushes for Grandad. All the time they laughed about that poor man and his homemade wings! Grandad then told her about his brother Leo playing for the town's cricket team as a young man on the grass pitch next to the hotel, before they packed up and started on their long cycle up into the countryside to the airfield at Brackla.

Chapter 11 – Preparing To Leave

The cycle up to Brackla was lovely. A sparkle of morning frost was still on the spider's webs at the side of the road. Shannon loved going anywhere with Grandad on his bike. He was such fun to be with and always seemed to be in a good mood and going up to Brackla was terrific. There were huge aeroplanes everywhere and Shannon even got to sit in them sometimes. They cycled alongside the tall fence of the airfield towards the big entrance gate. Inside were lots of amazing aeroplanes and people in various uniforms from different parts of the world. There were even a few exotic looking Indian men in turbans there today! Grandad stopped at the guardroom there and they went inside, where he had a joke or two with the men inside.

Soon, a tall, friendly man in a dark blue uniform walked into the room from outside and shook Grandad's hand. He had a strong accent and said to Grandad "Meester Makneel! *Nice to meet you. My name ees Karczewski, but please, call me Tadek! I take you to de plen. Eets not a very beeg jab!*" he joked. Shannon noticed a red and white striped badge on his shoulder and she knew that this meant that he was from Poland. She found Polish men's names to be so long and so strange – and how on earth to say them? The man looked down at Shannon with a friendly smile. "*Hallo Kochanie! Ent wot ees your name*?" "Shannon" she said. "*Ent you're here to help your Grended den? All right, cam wees me den ent we'll go ent see dis aeroplane.*" he held out his hand to Shannon's and Grandad pushed the bike beside them as they walked over to an aeroplane that looked very familiar to Shannon "*Wow – a Spitfire!*" she gasped excitedly. Tadek grinned in delight at her excitement "*Yes, det's right Shennon. You ees goot et knowing aeroplanes!*" Shannon had seen pictures of Spitfires before and sometimes seen them flying high overhead, doing stunts and loops above the town, but she'd never actually seen one up close before. Grandad laid his bike down on the grass, close to the Spitfire and started to get the paints sorted out, as Tadek took Shannon right up to the aeroplane. When Grandad turned round again he got a big shock indeed! There was Tadek stood on the edge of the wing, showing Shannon how the aeroplane controls worked inside as she sat *right* inside the pilot's seat with a flying helmet on and a smile that beamed right across her face. "Well look at you Shannon!" said Grandad. Shannon grinned proudly, glad that Grandad had seen her like this. Tadek turned to Grandad "I hope you ees ok dat I put Shennon to seet in de plane Meester Makneel?" Grandad just laughed "Put it like this Tadek, looking at Shannon's smile I don't think that I'd be too popular with her if I asked you to take her out of the seat just now!" he joked. "And call me Jimmy!" "All right – Jeemy!" Tadek laughed. Tadek turned to Shannon again "Now I talk to your Grendet about de painting of dees plane. You jus' seet here ent enjoy de view Shennon, all right?" Shannon just nodded, very happy to be left to sit in the pilot's seat of a Spitfire. Tadek took out a plan of the aeroplane from his pocket and showed Grandad which parts of the plane needed to be painted before he left. Shannon just sat very happily up there in the pilot's seat, looking around all of the small clocks and dials inside, as Grandad painted away below her. Normally Shannon would help Grandad out and chat with him, but Grandad knew that she was delighted to be up in such a special place and left her to enjoy being up there today.

After Grandad had almost finished he lifted Shannon down again to the ground. She looked at Grandad's work. He'd done a great job. "Well, we'd best get going soon Shannon. But I want to show you something first". He took her to the end of one of the wings and pointed at it. "You notice anything familiar Shannon?" She didn't know what he meant. "Look *really* closely just under the very tip of the wing Shannon". She looked under and saw it.

"Stardust, there!" she pointed.

"That's right Shannon. Some of these planes are up so high that they might just catch some stardust, like this one. You only see it because you believe in it. It's invisible to anyone else.

"Grandad, is it just our planes that get the stardust on them, then?" asked Shannon.

 Grandad put down his brush and looked up at Shannon, saying "I don't suppose so, Shannon. After all, it's not just 'our' planes, our ships, or our tanks or our men that are good. *Anyone* can be good. It doesn't matter where they come from, or what colour of clothes they're wearing. It just depends if they *want* to be good or not. I'm pretty sure that stars don't see the difference between what country something or someone's from. They just shine down on everyone, no matter what." He looked up at the side of the plane next to them again and said "It's just such a shame that such beautiful, amazing machines, with stardust on their wings have to be used to bomb and shoot at other people, on both sides of the war. It seems like such a waste." Grandad was staring at the ground, like he was thinking of something far away. He looked up at Shannon again quickly. "Right! That's this one done! Let's get going then!" as he pushed the bike back towards the Guardroom.

They met Tadek there again, who sat them down inside and gave them a nice cup of tea and some thick slices of bread, which were covered with fantastic slices of tasty sausage. Tadek pointed at the sandwich as the delicious tastes filled their mouths. " Eets Polish bret ent one of our men here makes de sausage heemself. No offence Jeemy, but bret ent sausage here ees jus' not de same!" he smiled. "Well Tadek…" replied Grandad, through a delicious mouthful. "I have to agree with you. That sausage was the best I've ever tasted!" With that Tadek asked Grandad and Shannon to wait a little while and he went out of the Guard-room. He came back two minutes later and handed Grandad a white paper wrapped parcel. Grandad peeped inside and saw three homemade Polish sausages and a few slices of Polish bread to take home! Tadek told him that his friends made it specially at the camp. Grandad smiled and thanked him and offered him his nice pen from his pocket in return, but Tadek refused to take it.

"No, please Jeemy. Ees a present. I like dat you like Poleesh foot, eet make me heppy!" Shannon smiled to herself because of Tadek's exotic accent – and thinking of eating Polish "foot!" Grandad wrote his address on a piece of paper and invited Tadek down to his and Granny's house some time. Tadek reached into his pocket and handed Shannon a present too. "End dees' a leetel sumseeng for' you Shennon." She looked in the bag and there were a few sweets and a small, wooden, painted doll. Shannon was delighted and thanked him. Tadek pointed at the doll and explained "De doll ees in the traditional costume for my area een Polant. I made eet years ago for my daughter. You remind me a beet of her." Shannon looked up at him "Is she back in Poland then…your daughter?" Tadek stared at the floor and sadness filled his eyes. He looked up again, his mouth smiling below his sad eyes and said "She like you to hev eet Shennon. I know you look efter eet." They continued to chat until the sun was starting to come down. As they went, Tadek said to Shannon "Please Shennon, I be very heppy eef you call me Wujek – eet means Uncle!" They thanked him again and cycled out of the airfield, waving back at Tadek as he waved to them, shouting "Do zobaczenia! Bye, bye!"

Soon they came to the top of the long, steep hill down to town. Grandad stopped the bike, facing down the hill. They looked at each other, knowing what was next! They always loved to scream their way down as they raced past the trees! "Right Shannon! It's been a great day, but now, I want you to give me the loudest scream that you possibly can as we rocket down the hill today – how about that?" Shannon grinned "Oh *yes* Grandad!" "Right Shannon" cried Grandad, slowly rocking the bike before they started down the hill "One....Two....Thrrrrreeeeeeeeeeeeeeeeeeee.....!" He pushed the bike off and it started to roll faster and faster! They screamed loudly with laughter as the wind pushed against their faces, their tummies tickled as the trees at the sides of the road whizzed past them!

Eventually the bike, their screaming and their laughter slowed and stopped round the corner at the bottom of the hill. A beautiful orange, red and yellow sunset to their left shone those colours on their faces and the trees around them. Grandad put his feet on the ground at each side of the bike and they both stared at the beautiful view. Shannon felt the small wooden doll in her pocket and thought of Tadek again – and his daughter. "Grandad, if you don't mind me asking....do you think that Tadek's daughter's dead? He looked very sad when I asked him about her?"

"I don't know Shannon" he replied, still looking above her at the sunset. "I know that in his country and in a lot of countries near his a lot of bad things are happening right now. So I imagine that there's a good chance that he won't see her again in this life." Shannon looked down at the doll "Oh the poor man....and the poor girl." she whispered. Grandad turned his head to look at her "Oh she'll be fine right now Shannon – don't you worry about that. There's something very important you have to learn Shannon. Possibly the most important thing to learn and believe of all, and it's this. If people look at, touch or hear each other they recognise something very familiar. And it's all too easy to think that what we see, hear and feel is all that we are. But our bodies are just what *carries* who we are in this world. You might call who we are our 'spirit' or our 'glow' – whatever you want. And our spirits are only being carried about on this world for a very short time. I look like an old man now, because the body that carries my spirit grows old and only lasts for so long. But I know that I'm not an old man inside! Like every spirit, I really don't have an age Shannon." he grinned. "I mean...how many old men scream their way down a hill on a bike at rocket-speed?" Shannon smiled at this. "Maybe a good way to think about it is this. Imagine presents that you've got - that you've waited for and really wanted. If you look back you might just see that the present was only really wonderful to play with for a short time. You got used to seeing it and maybe in time it broke and perhaps ended up getting chucked out. But if you look back and think about that present it wasn't the look of the present or what it did that really mattered. It was something that you can't touch – it was the happiness that it brought you. And that happiness is something that is always with you, which can't break and which can still make you smile today when you take the time to think about it. And it also brought such happiness to the person that gave you that present – and all that they got was to know that you loved it. But that was a wonderful gift to them too. So what we are isn't just what's seen and what slowly stops working Shannon. It's something so much more and something which lasts absolutely forever. So 'died' is a funny word Shannon. Who we are never dies at all, simple as that!

People will tell you different Shannon. But to me, believing that all that we are is just what we see, hear and feel is a crazy thing to believe. That is *real* blindness! Some people just *hope* that we're more. But I don't see the sense in just hoping. I'm quite happy to *know* and *believe* that who we are lives forever. It's just an obvious thing to me! So don't worry too much about people who have 'died' Shannon, they'll be very happy indeed where they are! Who we should be worried for are the people left behind who don't believe or who only hope. They are the people to feel sorry for." She looked up at him "I *think* that I understand Grandad!" "Well, I should hope so." he joked "It took me ages to say that and I don't want to say it all over again!"

They cycled, laughed and sang their way home and Grandad dropped her off at Mum's. When she got in she found Mum asleep on the armchair, the radio buzzing next to her. She looked comfy, so Shannon left her sleeping, turned off the radio and placed a blanket over her to keep her warm. Shannon went up to bed and took out the small, Polish doll to look at again. It made her think of Tadek and she wondered how and where his daughter was. She drifted slowly off to sleep.

Chapter 12 – The News

Shannon woke up and found Mum listening closely to the radio again. Today she was still quiet, tired and worried looking. But at least she talked a bit more today. Shannon asked her over breakfast what the matter was and Mum just answered that she wasn't feeling too good – but Shannon knew inside that there was something that Mum wasn't telling her. It made her so worried to see her Mum like that.

They went to church as usual. Today was the first time that she'd been back to church after finding out about the stardust, way up there above the altar on the 'Baldy Queen'! She couldn't help staring up there all the time, knowing what was hidden was so wonderful, so close, yet so unknown to everyone else there. The only time that she really looked down was when she heard a visiting old priest hilariously breaking wind very loudly on the altar, which echoed around the quiet church. Her friends Roy and Mark helped out the priest and they were all dressed up, kneeling in their robes on the altar in front of everyone. She saw them facing each other, their shoulders shaking trying to control their laughter from coming out, tears of laughter in their eyes. What made it all the funnier was that Shannon saw their Sunday School Teacher, Mrs Murray in the front row, staring hard and angrily at the boys as if to say 'How *dare* you smile in church!' All that Shannon could think to herself was '*I'll bet that God found that absolutely hilarious too!*'

Shannon never found out that day if Mrs Murray gave the boys a telling off at Sunday school as Mum took her straight home today. They normally stopped for tea, juice and a chat with her friends; so Shannon knew even more that Mum was very upset about something. Mum spent the rest of the day quite quiet and hardly left the radio's sound in the living room all day. Shannon just went up to her room and read a book for the afternoon. After a while she heard a knock at the front door downstairs. She went half way down the stairs to see Mum open the door and Granny come in. "Hi Granny!" shouted Shannon and raced down to the front door to give her a big hug. They chatted nicely, but then Mum asked Shannon if she would go upstairs again, because she and Granny had something private and important to talk about. Shannon went back upstairs to carry on with her book, a bit annoyed. But she wondered what they were talking about. It *must* be about what's been making Mum so sad, she thought. Soon she couldn't resist. She crept slowly down the edges of the stairs where she knew they were less creaky and listened, hardly breathing at the other side of the living room door. Soon she wished that she'd not come downstairs and listened at all. She could hear Mum crying like a baby. Granny was telling her things like "Don't be silly, it was just bad dream. Nobody's told or sent you anything to say that he's dead!"

Then Shannon heard Mum screaming things to Granny that made her stomach turn and tears stream down her face as she listened behind that door. "But I *saw* him! He was *there* in his uniform at the foot of my bed. He came to tell me he was gone. It was no dream! My Johhny's dead Mum! I *know* it! My husband's been killed by this *stupid* war and now my wee Shannon's not got a Father!"

Shannon burst the door open and ran in. Mum and Granny were holding each other, Mum's face puffy with tears. Both of them turned to her, shocked to see that she must have heard what they were saying. "It's *not* true Mum!" screamed Shannon "Daddy's *not* dead! You heard Granny, it was just a stupid dream!" All Mum could do was stare and then walk across the room towards Shannon, her arms out to hug her. But Shannon turned away from her and stormed out of the room, shouting "*No* Mum! It's not *true* and all you've gone and done is make everyone upset! Imagine believing a *dream!*" Then her tears started to flood down her face as she stomped upstairs to her room and fell onto her bed, crying hard into her pillow. Soon she felt a hand gently touching her shoulder. She turned and found Granny looking down at her, with such a sorry face. "Och Shannon, you're right my dear. Mummy just had a bad dream. I'm sure that your Dad's fine. I'm so sorry that you had to hear your Mummy say that." She leant down and hugged Shannon. That comforting smell of lavender and soap from Granny filled Shannon's nose. But she couldn't stop herself from crying. What if it was true? And why did Mummy think such a horrible thing up, just because of a dream? Granny just held onto her and stroked her hair as Shannon's tears ran into her pillow and she eventually fell asleep.

Shannon woke up and it was dark – she must have slept for hours. Her eyes and face were stingy with dried tears. It was so quiet. She took a piece of black paper down from the window and stared outside. She whispered up to the angels of the stars to take care of her Daddy wherever he was and to make it not true that he was gone forever. Soon she lifted her blanket to get into bed and found a folded note inside. It said:

'*My Dearest Little Shannon. Please don't worry. Wherever your Daddy is right now he wouldn't want you to be sad. Please don't be angry with Mummy, as she is only worried and loves you very much. Take care of her and see you very soon. Always with You. XXX Granny*'.

She held the note in her hand and lay on her side in the bed, staring up at the stars and slowly drifted back to sleep.

It was a slow journey to school for Shannon that morning. Her Mum had said sorry to her earlier and said that she was just being silly about a dream. Shannon wasn't sure whether to be angry, worried or both. She decided that she'd go down to the beach for a walk and go in late to school today. She needed to clear her head a bit. After a walk along by the sea she brushed the sand from her shoes and wandered back up the road to school and into her classroom, about half an hour late.

"Sorry I'm late Mrs Grant" she said "There was a very long army convoy of tanks and trucks and I couldn't get across the street." Mrs Grant seemed fine with this and just asked her to sit down. This wasn't an unusual excuse, as pupils were often late for that very reason. Mrs Grant carried on with her lesson for a little while and then suddenly stopped. A thought seemed to have come into her head and she stared angrily at Shannon. "Shannon McNeil!" she shouted. "Do you not live in Boath Terrace?" Shannon squeaked out a quick "Yes, Mrs Grant." Mrs Grant's face grew redder and her words echoed around the classroom walls as she shouted "Well Shannon! Unless the convoy of tanks and trucks was going across your garden path, it wouldn't have stopped you getting here in time, now would it? Because you *don't have to* cross any roads to *get* here, *do you*?" Shannon squeaked again, her head down "No Mrs Grant...!" Mrs Grant was now furious "*Right*, Shannon, stay behind after school and we'll see what to do with you for lying!" What a time Shannon was having- and it was only Monday!

At that very moment back home Shannon's Mum was making the most of a bit of winter sunshine by hanging out her washing in the garden. She was bending down to pick up a shirt from the washing basket when she saw the young soldier in kilted uniform slowly open the front gate. He carefully closed it behind him. She dropped the shirt and slowly stood up - and stared. He took his hat off and sighed. He had an envelope in his hand. She knew what he was here for. It seemed to her like he walked in slow motion as he stepped onto the garden path. Then he saw her standing by the washing line, staring at him. He'd had to do this a few times now and he could always tell when someone knew. He lowered his head and slowly walked across the grass and round the side of the house to Mum. He said quietly "Mrs McNeil? Your husband is John McNeil?" She couldn't speak and her face was still, as a cold tear trickled down over her pale cheek. Granny came outside and stood on the grass holding Mum's arm. "Yes" said Granny quietly. "She is Mrs McNeil and her husband is John McNeil" preparing for what he had to say.

The soldier coughed to clear his throat and faced Mum and gently said "Mrs McNeil, It is with deepest regret that I have to inform you that your husband Pte. John.G. McNeil, No. 552520 of The Seaforth Highlanders was killed in action on the night of…"

"I *know*!" said Mum, cold-faced, shaking and staring at him, before pointing to their upstairs bedroom window. "He came and told me already….up *there*! You can go now!" She quickly spun around and walked back towards the washing line, her arms hanging down by her sides as if in a dream.

"Mrs McNeil" said the young soldier after her "I'm *so* sorry, but please… take this telegram" She turned around and stared at him again and said

"All I know is that my husband and my daughter's father is gone for *nothing*! I don't need a *telegram* to tell me that." The soldier didn't know what to say, except.

"I'm sincerely so, so sorry Mrs McNeil."

"Isn't everyone?" she said and walked back slowly to the washing line. He posted the telegram through the front door and left with a heavy lump in his throat. This job never got any easier. Granny stood there in shock, watching him slowly disappear out the garden gate. It was like that for her when she got the news about her brothers all those years ago in the last war. But a thumping noise made her turn. Mum had fainted by the washing line. Granny ran to help.

Chapter 13 – Turning The World Upside-down

Sitting in the classroom Shannon's biggest worry right now was what punishment she was going to get after school. After a morning worrying about this, the lunchtime bell was a very welcome break. Shannon and Louisa decided to head down to the riverside to eat their snack on the grass and play on the rope-swing that they had put up on the tree over a pond by the big railway bridge. They were having great fun swinging over the weed-filled pond. But soon Louisa noticed Marjory, Veronica's bullying friend slowly walking their way along the riverside path. They knew that soon she'd probably push them about, take over the swing and very possibly even cut it down, but Louisa had a great idea. She quickly climbed up the tree to the branch where the rope of the swing was secured and untied it. "Good idea! said Shannon looking up at Louisa "If we take the rope she can't use it or cut it down!" But Louisa grinned as she lay across the thick branch "I've an even *better* idea, Shannon!" she giggled. Instead of climbing down with the rope, Louisa just flipped the rope loosely around the branch twice to make it *look* like it was tied and then let it hang down again. As Louisa climbed back down Shannon asked her what she was doing! "You'll see!" winked Louisa.

Sure enough, Marjory saw them and the swing and she marched across the grass towards them as Shannon and Louisa moved away from the rope-swing. "Well, well, well - a free swing!" shrieked Marjory as she walked towards them. It couldn't have worked better for Louisa. Marjory ran along the grass and threw herself at the rope, wishing to take charge of it. Shannon and Louisa stared, their mouths open as Marjory and the loose rope fell with a huge '*splash*!" into the weedy, ice-cold pond!

Marjory stood up, absolutely *covered* in slime and pond-weed and slowly stepped out of the stinky water, looking like a dripping swamp-monster! The girls burst into *hysterical* laughter at this and could hardly pick up their empty bottles and bag for laughing as they ran away across the grass! *Victory*! At this moment it didn't matter to them that not only Veronica, but also Marjory would be after them now. It was too funny to care about all that right now as they laughed their way across the grass, the 'swamp-monster' angrily, but slowly following far behind them!

But as they ran laughing a huge shape suddenly whooshed like a strong wind through the sky right in front of them! This made them stop and look up in amazement and forget all about 'The Swamp Monster'! Did they *really* see that? A German aeroplane had flown quietly past – right in front of them! They watched it circle around the big open fields and it came round in the sky in front of the girls again, over the trees. They could clearly see the pilot inside happily waving at them and other children as his plane slowly came down. They waved back. As the aeroplane's engines were silent, he'd probably just ran out of fuel and was just happy that the war was over for him. They knew a few German prisoners already who lived in the camp at the edge of the town. They were very friendly and sometimes gave out some excellent pieces of yummy, German chocolate to the children through the fence. Hopefully this one had a good chocolate supply on him too and he'd end up at the local camp, they thought. They also thought that they'd better tell someone though, so they went up to Mr McGregor's house nearby and told him. In less than a minute two army trucks came racing down the hill and onto the side of the field. Soon the plane glided down onto the football pitch by the river. The girls raced to get as close as they could and saw the pilot taken away by the local soldiers. Mr Sandcroft, the

Warden turned up and told Shannon and the other children that they'd best get back to school, which they did. Marjory, the 'swamp monster' stood by, who had long forgotten about getting the girls in all the excitement!

After school Shannon went to see Mrs Grant for her punishment from the morning. She was amazed when Mrs Grant told her that she wouldn't be getting a punishment after all because she said that Shannon had "helped capture a dangerous enemy by reporting his aeroplane coming down"! Shannon was a bit confused. All that she and Louisa had done was told old Mr McGregor about it, so that he could make sure that the man in the aeroplane was all right when he came down! Shannon said "Actually he didn't seem dangerous to us Mrs Grant, he waved at us and had a nice, handsome smile!" Mrs Grant didn't seem to like what Shannon had said. So rather than risk getting into trouble again, she just kept her mouth shut.

What a day again! Louisa and Shannon had a great, giggly walk home. Shannon still had a wide grin on her face as she wandered up her garden path. She was *desperate* to tell Mum about the aeroplane. It should really cheer her up. She hung up her coat and raced into the living room to tell Mum the 'news'. She was happily surprised to find that Granny and Grandad were there too. She gave them a happy 'Hello' and kissed them. She started to tell them excitedly about the aeroplane at lunchtime, but they all looked so serious and quiet, so she stopped. Nobody said anything. Shannon looked at them, still smiling and asked "What.....?". "Come here please Shannon Dear." Mum said. She could tell it really was something serious by their faces. Mum put her arms out as Shannon crossed the room and slowly sat on her lap on the armchair. She turned

102

to Shannon and looked her deep in the eyes, not saying a thing, but her eyes full of worry and sadness. Mum was finding it hard to say anything, so Shannon asked quietly "What is it Mum? What's wrong?" Mum sighed out loud and looked at the ceiling, then back down at Shannon and gently said " Oh Shannon, I've got to tell you my girl…..it's your Daddy. He's……he's not coming home Shannon…!" There was no sound for a few seconds. "What do you mean Mum? For Christmas, you mean?" Mum just stared at her and slowly shook her head, whispering "No Shannon…he's not coming home ever." She handed Shannon the telegram "A man brought this letter today Shannon. Your Daddy…he's……been killed fighting!" Shannon felt numb all of a sudden, like her whole body had just got an injection at the dentists. She just shook her head and stared back at Mum, then burst into tears as they hugged each other. Granny and Grandad came across and hugged them too, no words were spoken or needed.

Chapter 14 – Back to the Stars

Mum said that Dad's body wouldn't be coming back home. She just said it was best that way. Grandad had offered to take Shannon out for a long walk and maybe round to his house for the evening, as the priest was coming around to the house to arrange a memorial service for Daddy. Shannon had run out of tears. She hugged Mum and Granny as she left the house with Grandad. As she went out the front door she felt the cold air of the world outside – a world that she felt had totally changed since she got that terrible news. Walking along in the streets they met a few people that they knew who wanted to talk, but Shannon and Grandad didn't feel much like talking right now. So as they got close to the church and Grandad asked if she'd like to go in there and chat, Shannon agreed that it was a good idea.

Grandad opened up the church and they sat down in the front row. The only light was that small red glow from the lamp on the wall. They chatted about all sorts of things. Grandad reminded her about what he had said on the bike recently – that who we are isn't just what our bodies are. That we're something far more important and that we live forever and ever. But at this moment, Shannon found this harder to believe than anything else. It seemed so ridiculous an idea to her right now and just made her angry "Well Grandad, I don't think you're right!" she shouted, her words echoing around the empty church "*How* can you believe that? My Dad's *dead* Grandad! I can't hug him now, or see his smile, I'll never hold him again....I'll.....I'll!" she stood up and ran crying towards the back of the church, but stopped near the back door. She was so angry, but knew that Grandad meant well, no matter how stupid his ideas seemed right now. He slowly walked up behind her and put his hand on her shoulder. She turned round with her head down and they hugged, as Grandad whispered "Oh my dear, wee Shannon. I don't blame you for not believing that who we are lives forever – and now is the hardest time of all to believe that. It's far easier to hope at a time like this." She just hugged him tighter until he said "Let's go up to the stars tonight Shannon – let's do it for your Daddy, eh?" She nodded.

Grandad took the ladder in from the back of the church and he asked Shannon to hold it at the bottom as he stood it up against the sides of the baldequino high above the altar, just as she had seen Tuppence do a few nights before. She saw the glow from the galley ships in the window and picture at the far end of the church shining towards the tin that Grandad took down and smiled, thinking 'I wish Daddy could have seen this…just once!' Grandad came down and she looked into the tin – her face lighting up again with that amazing golden glow. There were more clouds about tonight, so the streets were darker, the moonlight struggling to shine through. They walked down the road to the museum and Grandad opened the back door. In the darkness she could *just* make out the bike, complete with the wings attached. They pushed it slowly out onto the grass and Grandad had a quick puff on his pipe before saying "Right then. Let's get going Shannon." She wandered to the box-trailer at the back, but Grandad said "And where do you think *you're* going Shannon?" She was confused "But I thought we were going up tonight Grandad…?" "Oh, we *are* going up Shannon, but *you're* driving, I'll get in the box-trailer. I need to know that you can drive this thing too, you know!" Shannon couldn't believe it. "But I don't know how to Grandad!" He smiled "There's nothing to know Shannon. Here's a jar of stardust. Keep it safe in your pocket now. When you're ready to go, dip your finger into it and touch a little bit of it onto the tips of the wings. The wings will flap, you pedal and up we go. When it starts to get hard to breathe, take a pinch more stardust and throw it in the air above us and we'll be fine - simple!" "Simple!" she replied. But Grandad just nodded and handed her his goggles from the handlebars. "You've been chosen as a Starcarer Shannon and only Starcarers can make this fly and no-one else. The only thing that you've got to learn is the confidence in yourself that you can. Here's my cap – put it on to keep your hair from flying everywhere. I just wear it to keep my head warm!" he joked. "Go on my girl - just believe!" With that he walked round to the box trailer and climbed in, putting his hands behind his head and his feet up on the edge of the trailer behind Shannon. He put the spare goggles on and Shannon sat on the bike seat. "Well…?" he said "…what are we waiting for my girl?" With that she reached into her jacket and opened the glowing jar of stardust. She dipped the tip of her finger in, which tickled. She wiped some on each wingtip, which glowed white and started to flap. "It's working!" she said "Of *course* it is Shannon!" Grandad replied. The flapping got quicker and suddenly the bike started to move forwards, slowly getting faster as it bumped along the rough grass as Shannon pedalled. She didn't have to pedal much at all, but she did anyway to make her feel more balanced. The trees got closer, Shannon thought that it wouldn't take off! But Grandad shouted from the back "Do it for your Dad, Shannon!" With that, as soon as Shannon thought of Dad again the bike swooped up into the skies. "*Wooohhooooooo!*" yelped Grandad with delight from the back as they climbed into the night sky above the frost-twinkling ground below them. Shannon turned and smiled at him, but then she felt guilty to be smiling so soon after getting that terrible news about Daddy. As if knowing exactly what she was thinking, Grandad shouted "You keep smiling my girl. He wants you to and is so proud of you right now!" With that she smiled again and looked up into the skies above them, then asked Grandad "You never said which way to go Grandad – and how do I steer?" "To the moon!" he replied. "You steer with what's *inside* you Shannon. Just want to go to a place that you're looking at and you will, just like you did with the galley in the painting before." She looked up to the right towards the moon. As she did so, the wings turned the bike straight towards it. Through the clouds they went, soon becoming like scattered blankets of cotton wool below them. She felt the air become hard to breathe, but soon remembered what to do. She threw a pinch of stardust up above them and suddenly it was warm and her breathing became easy and clear again. The wings now glowed that wonderful gold. They flapped slower and quieter as they moved them forwards through space, straight for the glowing moon. It was so peaceful again. She didn't know why, but she was beginning to feel almost happy, even after getting such terrible news today. She found it strange that she felt like Dad was somehow with her, way up there, much more than she ever did when he was away fighting. She looked back towards Grandad and smiled as she saw him puffing away on his pipe. He winked at her "Grand job my wee Shannon!"

She had to ask him something "Do you never worry about falling off the bike Grandad? Being lost out here in space?" He laughed. "Watch this Shannon!" With that Grandad stood up and threw himself out of the back of the trailer and slowly started to float away from her into space! He spun himself round, laughing and making smoke circles around himself with his pipe. Shannon panicked and screamed. "Grandad!" With that the golden wings turned the bike around, swooped towards Grandad and gently caught him in the trailer, a smile still across his face. Shannon was so glad! "Your bike, it *rescued* you Grandad!" "Not at all Shannon, it was *you* who 'rescued' me! I trust in you." Shannon didn't know what he meant. "Shannon, it's like this. You didn't want me to float away into space and be lost in this darkness forever, because you love me. Now I could have just wanted the bike to come to me and it would have. But I wanted you to see that *you* can do it. You saw me fall out and *your* love wanted me rescued. This bike just listened to that and did what *you* wanted." He pointed his pipe over her shoulder "So do you want to go to there!" he smiled.

Soon they were swooping down to land on the moon, next to Uncle Angus's house again. He came out as they landed. As Angus got to the garden gate he looked delighted "Oh my goodness! *You're* driving tonight Shannon, and hardly a bit of moondust anywhere. You could teach your Grandad a thing or two about landing!" He hugged her and turned to Grandad curiously "And I wasn't expecting you tonight" he said. "Grandad stepped out of the box-trailer and turned to 'Angus', a serious look on his face. "No Angus. We've not really got stars to do tonight. We're up for a different reason. I'm afraid that Shannon's Mum got a telegram today…" Angus turned back to Shannon "Oh my poor child. I'm so, so sorry!" as he put his hand on her shoulder. The sadness of the day caught up with Shannon again and she burst into tears. Angus put his hand round her shoulder and led her into the house, followed by Grandad. They went into the living room "Sit yourself down here Shannon" said Angus, leading her into his comfy armchair. He patted her shoulder and said "I'll go and get us all something to drink" and he and Grandad went through to the kitchen to talk to each other quietly and leave her in peace for a while. Like Grandad, Angus was a nice man that knew when it was best not to say or ask too much.

To any other child at any other time, being up here on the moon amongst the stars would fill them with amazement and such happiness. Shannon was no different. But today, even amongst all of these amazing things, she felt numb, dark and sad inside. Dad was gone, that's all she knew. And right now even a trip to the moon couldn't take away that sadness and feeling of 'loss'. But if today's news made it the worst day she had ever had, tonight would turn out to be the most incredible - and the best so far!

Chapter 15 – That 'Special' Star!

Grandad and Angus had been chatting for a while in the kitchen. Shannon had looked up for a while at the picture of the castle and the galley over the fireplace, but the sadness that she felt had just made her sit there, so alone. They walked in with their teapot and cups rattling and sat at the table by the window. Angus carried a bottle of sugarelly for Shannon. He looked over at her and carefully asked "Would you like to come over here and sit with us Shannon?" She wiped her tears, wandered over to the table and sat down next to Grandad. He had put the framed, old newspaper clipping of him and his brothers in uniform on the table. There was also a strange piece of shiny, twisty metal on the table too. "Shannon, your Grandad and I have had a little chat in the kitchen." said Angus gently. "We know how sad you are about the news that you got about your Daddy and that you'll feel that you've lost him forever. So we feel that now is the time to tell you something very important indeed. " He looked nervously at Grandad and then took the newspaper clipping in the frame and held it up for Shannon to see. "Your Grandad told me that he showed you this at the war memorial recently and that he told you that the pictures around the side of the clipping were of his brothers." "Yes Uncle Angus." she replied "But by the look on your face and the way that you're talking you sound like you're going to tell me it's not true though?" But Angus just smiled as he slowly shook his head "Oh no, Shannon! It's very true what he said. The only thing is ….your Grandad and I didn't want you to get frightened when you learnt who I *really* am."

Shannon looked confused "What do you mean Uncle Angus?" He handed her the frame. "Here Shannon - read carefully what it says about the man in the middle picture on the left". She took the frame and read "Well, it's a picture of Grandad's brother Leo, when they were young. And the newspaper clipping says that he was in the 'RHA' – but I don't know what that is." "Royal Horse Artillery Shannon" replied Angus immediately. He lifted the twisted, shiny metal thing from the table. "And do you know what this is?" he asked her. She looked, not knowing what it was, but it had the name 'Reulach' scratched neatly onto it. "I don't know" she said, as she handed it back to him. "Well, it's a horses' bit Shannon, the bit that goes in the mouth. And that's why I've got it. It's from my horse" he said. Shannon was confused. "I still don't know what you mean Uncle Angus." He looked at Grandad and back to Shannon, slowly and carefully said "Shannon…it's like this. I'm not Angus. Angus is my Daddy's name. He's the man in the middle of this newspaper clipping. But….I'm *Leo* - I'm really your Great-Uncle. Your Grandad here's my brother." She pushed herself back in her chair, shaking her head. "But Leo died before I was born – you can't be!" She turned to Grandad, who nodded and said "It's true Shannon, but don't be afraid." Leo stood up and looked out of the window, before turning back to Shannon and said "It's a strange word that is used down there on Earth - 'died'. It's so final, so sad, so….well…wrong! I've got a nice stone down there with my name on it. My family and friends put lovely flowers in front of it. But it's really only for people down there. Maybe it's like the stars up here. Your Grandad shows them respect by coming up here and caring for them. You might think that they'd be all right without him really, yet at the same time that showing of love he gives to the stars is *so* important." Shannon couldn't help staring, wondering if this was all true. Grandad joined in, saying "I've told Shannon all about our spirits. Who we really are that lasts forever."

He turned back to Shannon " Your Uncle Leo here was given the honour of caring for the moon when his spirit left the Earth. You see him looking like he does when he lived down on Earth, because *your* spirit chooses to let your eyes see him that way." Shannon couldn't help staring at Uncle Leo now. He smiled and sat down opposite her, grabbed her bottle of sugarelly, shook it up and down and poured it into a glass in front of her as she watched. "Now Shannon, could someone not *'alive'* do *that*?" Her face changed and she stood up, suddenly looking *very* angry. "Why are you doing this?" And you too, Grandad? You're just trying to tell me that Angus here is your brother to try and prove that we all really live *forever*! You're just doing it because you pity me because my Dad's dead! As I said in the church, he's gone forever and that's *that*!" She sat back down, her tears starting to flow again.

Grandad and Leo stayed quiet, until Leo pushed the metal horse's mouth-bit across the table to her again, saying softly "Shannon, perhaps you need something to help you believe, especially today. Your Grandad tells me that you like horses? And your Grandad and I think that you should visit one particular star tonight. A star that you'll hopefully find will be very special indeed to you. And you'll need this bit if you want to take my horse!" What was he talking about? She answered him angrily, as he stood up and opened the window "You haven't even *got* a horse! When we landed here we could see for miles. There's nothing but dust and rocks out there! Do you *really* expect me to believe…" But she suddenly stopped. A beautiful brown horse with a white mark on his forehead had put his head through the open window into the sitting room and was being petted by a grinning Uncle Leo. He turned round "I'm sorry Shannon, you were saying..?" he grinned. He turned back to the horse and stroked it's head as he said to it "Well Reulach, this is my Great

Niece and she's called Shannon. Say hello!" The horse nodded his head and snorted. Shannon stood up, amazed. "Reulach?" she asked "Is that the horse that used to care for the stars with Grandad's Daddy? The flying one?" He nodded back "And my Daddy too Shannon. Yes - this is Reulach." He turned back to the horse. "Are you ready to take this nice wee girl to visit that special star, then?" Reulach nodded again, then walked away to stand next to Grandad's bike, outside the garden. Grandad stood up and put his hand out to Shannon "Well, my girl. Are you coming or not?" he smiled. She jumped up and they all went outside and stood next to Reulach and the bike on the moondust. Leo took a saddle and all sorts of straps with him, to prepare the horse for the journey. Grandad was over at his bike, getting ready to go too.

Leo spoke as he put the saddle and straps on, as Shannon stroked Reulach's head. "This is a very special horse Shannon. I want to tell you just how special she is. When me and your Grandad and our brothers were young men, a terrible war came on. We were only boys really, but we thought that it would be brave to volunteer to go and fight and to get a nice uniform and some money for nice things too. I joined something called The Royal Horse Artillery, purely because they had horses; and I always *loved* horses. The night before I went, the angels woke me up and they brought my Daddy's horse Reulach back from the stars to look after me and to keep me safe in battle. And that's just what she did. You're too young to know how terrible things were in that war. But the one thing that I'll say is that I, your Grandad, all of our brothers and just about every man who was fighting on any side really wanted was some peace and to be with his family, that's all. And we soon learnt that no person is bad just because of what country they're from, or just because someone else says that they are. Reulach helped me to know this and was here by my side through those dark times. I'll tell you Shannon, I remember a wet and muddy night. It was Reulach and my first ever time in battle. We were riding through a huge noise of bombs and fizzing bullets, trying to get back to safety. I could see almost nothing in all of the choking smoke, splashing mud and dark rain. As we galloped along a whistling bomb suddenly landed with a boom very close to us! I was thrown off Reulach and I landed in a pool of cold, dark mud. Now that mud wasn't like any old mud. It was deep, heavy and thick. It dragged you down into it's wet darkness. I sunk until my head went under and I struggled hard, trying to get back to the surface, but it was no use. The more I struggled the more I sank. I'd almost given up hope when I felt a hand grabbing mine and fixing a strap around my wrist. Then I felt myself being pulled upwards. I came to the surface and gasped for air. As my eyes opened I saw the figure of a man in the darkness above me, moving Reulach backwards to pull me out and save me. Soon I was out of that thick, muddy pool and lying on my back, with all the noise still going on around me and the stranger who saved my life was lying down next to me in all that dirt and noise, exhausted."

Leo stopped preparing Reulach for a moment and his eyes seemed to be thinking of something far away. "I got my breath back and sat up on that dark, muddy ground to thank this man who saved my life and found to my amazement that he was supposed to be my enemy. He was a German soldier, but he was just another human being mixed up in all of that senseless noise and mud and horror with the rest of us. But I soon saw that he was also very badly hurt. He'd saved my life, the life of someone supposed to be his enemy, yet these were the last moments of his life. I could speak some German from what I had learnt at school and I thanked him as best as I could. He gave me an envelope from his pocket and asked me to keep it. He must have known that his time on Earth was almost up. But he suddenly looked up at the skies above us, amazed and smiling. He kept talking about "wonderful singing" and I knew that the angels were singing for him to welcome such a good man up to the stars. I held his hand as I watched his body slowly stop working, a wide and very happy smile still on his darkened face." Leo looked at Shannon and noticed a tear running down her face. "Oh my dear" he said "I'm so sorry Shannon, I should have thought before telling you a story about war on such a day." But Shannon just gently wiped her tear away and smiled as she continued to stroke Reulach's forehead "Oh, that's all right Uncle Leo. It was lovely that you told me. What happened next though?" He patted Reulach's back "Well, I gave this lovely horse here here a big thank you and hug for helping to pull me out, climbed back onto my saddle and we got out of there as fast as we could! Reulach really looked after me during the war. When the war finished I rode her home to my Mother's house. She was so glad to have a son back safe. But the next night that I had to go star-caring the angels told me that it was time for Reulach to stay back up in the stars and they took me back home themselves. I only saw her again once I got given this job here - of looking after the moon. I had opened the envelope that the German man had given me that night on that muddy, dark field and there was a picture inside of a small girl. Her name was Gabriela and the man who saved my life was her Father. I saved up some money to go to the German man's house after the war finished. I met his family, including little Gabriela. I found out that his name was Siegfried Fischer. His family were so nice to me and were so proud to find out about the goodness that he showed to me, back on that muddy, dark field. They were just like our own family. I wrote to them many times over the years and we always sent each other Christmas cards."

Leo had finished preparing Reulach "Right then Shannon! I know that you've ridden horses before, so let's get you up on her then." He helped Shannon get up onto Reulach and Grandad pushed his bike close to them. Leo stood down by her side "Now, Shannon, because Reulach lives up in the stars she doesn't need any stardust to fly. All you have to do is think in your head which way you want to go, or whether you want to go slower or faster and Reulach will understand". Shannon looked ahead. There were millions of stars up there. She asked "But Uncle Leo, which one is the 'special' star that you were talking about? And what am I supposed to find there?" He laughed "Well how am I supposed to know which star it is Shannon? And what are you supposed to find there? Well that's up to you to find out. Just keep thinking of your Dad and you'll get there, trust me!" He walked round to the front of Reulach and kissed her forehead, then looked back up at Shannon. "You can go now Shannon. Have a wonderful time. I truly hope that you find what you're looking for." With that Shannon looked ahead and imagined in her mind Reulach trotting forward….and she did! Next she imagined her galloping…and they were! And next, she imagined Reulach swooping up into the skies and she heard Leo behind shouting "Have a good trip!" as they swooped up into the twinkling skies in a shower of sparkling, golden stardust. She looked behind and saw Grandad following on his bike and the moon quickly growing smaller behind them. This was *the* best way anyone could *ever* ride a horse she thought, her smile beaming. She remembered what Uncle Leo had said about thinking about Dad to get her to that 'special' star. So she closed her eyes and thought of Dad and Mum laughing back at their house, which made her grin. Her eyes opened and there in the distance, out of all of the millions of stars was one that she just *knew* deep inside was the special one. A silvery web appeared, pointing straight at it. It looked like almost every other star she could see! She had no idea why it was that one, what was special about it or why she was going there. All she did know was that she couldn't *wait* to find out!

Chapter 16 – The Most Wonderful Discovery

Reulach glided so beautifully through that peaceful, black, twinkling space. Grandad was riding his bike alongside her and they chatted all about Shannon's Daddy and about wonderful times that they'd had with him. It was a journey of tears and laughter. Tonight of all nights, Shannon just couldn't help thinking of her Daddy. So with thoughts of him so strong in her mind, Reulach stayed on course, straight for 'that' star. As they got very close to the star Shannon laughed and turned to look at Grandad. She'd heard him singing a song that her Daddy used to sing to her 'When the Red, Red Robin comes Bob-Bob-Bobbing along!' But as she looked at Grandad, she was shocked to see that his mouth wasn't moving at all, yet she still heard the song! And now she knew that it sounded just like her Daddy singing. Grandad turned to her and smiled as she said. "Grandad….do you hear that?". Grandad just grinned back at her, the glass on his goggles twinkling the reflection of the star ahead. "Hear what Shannon?" She felt a bit silly now "Well, it might sound daft Grandad, but I am pretty sure that I can hear singing and it sounds like my Daddy!" "Really? Next you'll be telling me that your Grandad has a flying bike that he takes to the moon!" he laughed. With that, Reulach started to slow down as they glided to a stop next to the star, resting on the silvery web. As they slowed down, Shannon heard the singing slowly stop.

Grandad got off his bike and gave Reulach a sugar-lump "Reulach loves these sugarlumps, just as much as *you* love sugarelly!" as he helped Shannon down from Reulach's back. They both turned and faced the star, looking up and down at it's warm, golden glow. "So here we are then Shannon!" said Grandad. Shannon suddenly realised that she felt a bit silly. They'd come all this way and she didn't know why! She waited for Grandad to say something, but he didn't. "Grandad, sorry but….what do we do now?" she asked. She was surprised by his answer "Well I don't know Shannon….you took us her!" he smiled. Now she felt really silly. "I'll tell you what Shannon. Let's just sit down for a while and enjoy the view, eh?" He rustled about in his jacket pocket, took out a small paper bag and held it out to Shannon "Fancy a mint?" She took one and they both sat down on the thread, slurping away at the sweets with their legs dangling below them facing the distant Earth.

Shannon noticed the sun, far beyond and wondered about it "Grandad, is the sun a star too?" "Of course Shannon! It's a very big one though!" he grinned. "And whoever put that sun there made it that way for a very, very good reason. Everyone knows that nothing that's called 'life' down on Earth can survive without that one star. And that's also why the Earth turns, going dark at sunset to light at sunrise. It's to show people on Earth that they should trust that when it seems that life and light goes away that they should never panic or be too sad…because it's always there and always comes back again. It's a lesson that's repeated thousands of times in most peoples lives, yet even the most 'intelligent' of people never notice it, or think about it for themselves. For example Shannon, is every day sunny?" Shannon scrunched up her nose and turned to him, as if it was a daft question "Of course not Grandad, that's daft!" He said "But Shannon, *every* day is sunny!" She looked confused, remembering so many cold and wet ones. Grandad smiled and continued "It is always a sunny day Shannon, because the sun is *always* there. Clouds and rain might be in the way and make things seem miserable. But if you look beyond the clouds, just lift yourself a bit and you'll find that the sun shines as bright and warm as ever." Shannon looked at him, not quite understanding and thinking that she'd been 'caught out' by a clever riddle. He saw her confusion and laughed as he held out the small paper bag again. "Don't worry Shannon, you'll understand it all one day. Here, have another mint".

There was silence for a while as they both sat, admiring the view and watching the odd shooting star *whoosh* past them. Shannon looked down at the Earth, where France was, covered by the shadow of night right now. That place on the Earth seemed so dark, so far away to her. To her, right then, it only meant where Dad was killed. Grandad noticed her looking sad again and said gently "I know that you miss him Shannon, but do you believe that you'll see him again?" She whispered "I really don't know Grandad" as she felt her tears starting to flood her eyes. Grandad nodded his head towards Earth and said "Look down there Shannon. So many people see their loved ones going away from there and they never get the chance to believe in the magic of all that's up here! Most only get hope or anger, or a mix of the two. Look at the last place your Dad was down there. A muddy field, far away from home." He turned to her "But Shannon, knowing all that your Daddy is, do you *really* believe that what happened to him down there stopped him forever?" She turned to him again and whispered "I don't know Grandad. I really wish that I could believe that I'll see him again, but it's so hard to…!" A thought came to her head. "Grandad, when we go back down to Earth later tonight, can we please stop down by France, so that I can see where he was? Maybe see if they've put a small stone up for him with his name on it?" But Grandad just took her hand and stood her up, saying "Shannon, why are you wanting to look in the muddy ground down there for your Daddy?" she couldn't answer that, but felt disappointed that he didn't seem to understand why she wanted to go there. He put his arm around her

"Look, I know that you might feel so far from him now – further from him than you've ever felt before. Maybe you need something to help you relax, to cheer you up. Now you brought us to this star, so I think that we should at least do something now that we're here, don't you?". She nodded and they both turned around to face the glow of the star in front of them again. "Now Shannon, close your eyes and think happy thoughts." She closed her eyes and tried to, but all she could think about today was her Dad and the sadness of him being gone. She heard Grandad saying again "Happy thoughts Shannon. Happy times with your Dad" She thought of her Daddy laughing with Mummy back at home as she stood there. Then a smile crept warmly across her face as she imagined her Daddy singing his 'Red, Red Robin' song again, but she kept her eyes shut. She thought to herself that the singing must just be in her head, but she was just happy to hear it again anyway. Through the singing she heard her Grandad beside her saying "Put your hand out Shannon, towards the star." The singing stopped, but at this star she felt so close to her Daddy again and all sadness had disappeared for that moment. With her eyes still closed she slowly put her hand forward in front of her, expecting to feel just the glowing warmth of the star. But instead, as she reached into the star she felt a wonderful and strong wave of tingling happiness rush all over her. She jumped slightly as another hand in the star gently took hers and she quickly opened her eyes. She started to make out the shape of a face in the glow. She thought that it must be an angel again, but the hand and face somehow seemed familiar to her. She felt herself being gently pulled forwards and without thinking she stepped into the glow of the star!

Suddenly she found herself surrounded by a beautiful light and then felt familiar arms around her, hugging her as she burst into tears of intense happiness. She felt a finger on her chin, raising her face to look up. And there he was....smiling down at her....*Daddy*! He lifted her up and they hugged each other more tightly than they probably ever had before and he whirled her around in that wonderful light. She *never* knew that happiness could be like this, so incredible! But now, she believed! This was no dream. "My wee, beautiful Shannon" said Daddy "It's so wonderful to see you again." She couldn't help staring at him, smiling back at her. She touched his face. How could this be? Daddy died in the war, but it seemed like he knew what she was thinking "Oh Shannon, don't think of how strange it all seems. You're not dreaming, my wee princess. We go on forever! Isn't it fantastic?" he grinned. She felt his arms around her again and she snuggled her face to his neck and kissed him, not letting go.

She didn't know how long she hugged him for, but she knew it was all so real. He was so *alive*! Eventually she heard him whisper "It's time to go princess – for now." She felt him kiss her gently on the forehead and then she saw that glorious light turning into dark, sparkling space as he gently placed her down outside the star again. She looked back to the light, still seeing his face in that golden glow and shouted out "But I don't want to go Daddy- I want to stay with you!" She saw him smile back "Oh Shannon, it's not your time yet. *You* can see me again up here. You're a Starcarer. I'm *so, so* proud of you! But there's something *very* important that I want you to remember Shannon. In your life down there on Earth, *try* to be as *good* to other people and to yourself as you can. Trust what you feel deep inside of you and let other people do and be what they want, as long as it doesn't harm anyone else. The better you are down there, the easier it will be for you to come through the star all by yourself one day. *Please* Shannon, just try your best, my wee Princess, that's all you can do." She nodded and his hand came out of the star and stroked her face. "As I said when I was down on Earth Shannon - I'm *always* with you. Now I *know* it Princess. That was a good 'guess' I had eh?" He smiled as he blew her a kiss. His face started to disappear back into the brightness of the star again as he said "Take care Shannon. 'See you soon. Take care of your Mum until I see her again, when it's her time..." and he was gone!

She just stood there, staring into the golden glow, until she heard Grandad say next to her "*Now* you know why we care for the stars Shannon. They're doors to our loved ones. You're so lucky to have the privilege of seeing that already." Shannon's eyes lit up "Grandad, this is fantastic! I can take Mum up here to see him, she's missing him so...." "*No* Shannon!" said Grandad. "If you try to tell her, she won't possibly believe you and you'll just make her more upset. You *can't*! She'll see him again when it's time, like your Dad said to you just now. But *not now* Shannon!" She could see that he meant it. "Shannon, I'm so delighted that you're a Starcarer, that you got to know that we go on forever - it's *such* an *amazing* thing! But when you are lucky enough to get to know these things when you're still living on Earth you also have a huge responsibility to protect these secrets. Even keeping them secret from our own families, for everyone's sake. Do you understand?" Shannon nodded – she was still amazed and glowing with delight about having met her Daddy again.

They flew to Uncle Leo's on the moon and left Reulach with him, before continuing their flight back home on Grandad's bike. Shannon was so excited and talked about Daddy all the way back. And Grandad was so glad to see her happy again, for her to have had the chance to see for definite that her Daddy and all of us go on forever. He had to try to calm her down as she almost screamed with excitement about it to him at the museum as they put the bike away. Shannon started to think about all of the relatives from the past she could meet now.

When they got to Shannon's Mum's house it was past midnight. Mum and Granny were still sitting quietly in the living room, staring into the fire. They hardly noticed the door open. Grandad made an excuse, saying that they went for a long walk along the beach and then to his house for a chat and games of cards, which they seemed to be all right about. He made some tea and they sat for while and then he and Granny hugged Mum and they left to walk back to their house. But as he and Granny walked down the road he wondered whether or not Shannon could keep these secrets that she found out or not. He didn't want to see Shannon's Mum upset or to risk other people finding out how to get to the stars and then maybe they might treat them badly. He had to trust her to do what's right. After all, she was chosen to be a Starcarer and she wouldn't have been chosen if she couldn't keep a secret, surely! But back at the house they'd just left, she looked at Mum's face, red and puffy with tears, thinking that she'd lost her husband forever. Shannon was almost bursting inside, wanting to tell Mum so much.

Chapter 17 – The Christmas Dance

The next few days were quiet and dark. Shannon wasn't at school and tomorrow was the day of the church memorial service for Daddy. There were just a handful of days to go to Christmas, but no decorations were put up, no radio was put on and the only sounds were of sympathy cards being put through the door and falling into the lobby. It was so frustrating for Shannon. She *knew* that Daddy was safe, alive and more happy than she'd ever seen him – and in such a wonderful place. She was more happy for him than she could possibly say, but yet here was Mum sitting so full of sadness, thinking that she'd never see Daddy again. It all seemed so unfair to Shannon. She was '*dying*' to tell her, but knew that if she did that Mum couldn't possibly believe her and it would only make matters worse. The school Christmas Dance was on that night. Shannon really wanted to go, but didn't want to upset Mum by going or talking about it. Thankfully Granny came round to see them and told Mum she thought that it was a good idea that she went. Mum nodded that she thought so too. Granny even took round a lovely purple velvet dress that she'd made for Shannon to wear. She helped her get ready and put her hair in a lovely plait, with a flowery hair-band to hold it in place. Shannon walked downstairs and into the living room to show Mum. She stood in front of her, smiling and with her arms out at her sides, waiting for a reaction. "Well?" said Granny, behind Shannon "What do you think of this lovely little lady then?" But Mum just burst into tears again and wrapped her arms around Shannon, saying "Oh, you're so beautiful Shannon. If only your Dad could have seen you right now!" Shannon just thought to herself 'But he *can* see me!' Mum moved back, but still holding her and smiled through her tears. "You have a *wonderful* time tonight Shannon!"

Grandad came round to walk Shannon to the school. When he came in and saw her in the hallway he just said a quick "Hello!" and walked right past her, then said loudly to Granny in the sitting room "There's a beautiful Princess out in the hallway Granny...has she come round to play with Shannon?" Shannon smiled and Grandad looked back into the hall, winked at her and whispered "You look absolutely fantastic Shannon – a proper little lady! Come on, let's get going then". He held out his arm and started talking in a funny, posh accent, his nose pointing to the ceiling". *My good lady, might I have the wonderful pleasure of accompanying your good self to the dance*?" She smiled and they went out the door and walked arm in arm down the road towards the school.

Grandad walked into the school with her and to the door of the gym, where the party was. The door was open and they could see lots of children, balloons, paper chains and the Christmas tree glowing in the far corner. He wished her a wonderful time and left to walk back home. Shannon walked in and as she did all of the children stared at her. Most stayed away. She knew what they were thinking – 'Her Dad's dead'. It wasn't that they were being nasty, it was just that they didn't know what to say. Mrs Grant came across with tinsel wrapped around her hair. She had obviously heard the news too, as she looked down sadly at Shannon. "Oh Shannon, I'm so glad that you could come. Are you all right?" Shannon smiled "I'll be fine Mrs Grant, thank you." Then she noticed that Louisa had come up to talk to her. She looked beautiful too, in her pink skirt and top. Her bottom lip was shaking and she started to cry, hugging Shannon "Oh Shannon, I'm so, so sorry about your Daddy!" she wailed. Shannon hugged her back. She was such a good friend – and if only she knew that Shannon's Dad was absolutely fine, high up above them in the stars, right now. She patted Louisa's back and thanked her.

Soon the dancing started. The boys sat on benches at one side of the room and the girls on the other, until they all had to go up and choose their partners for the dances. John Cunningham was the first to choose Shannon that night. This was no bad thing, as he was probably the best dancer in their year. This was always a nervous time and even the most confident girls and boys there were nervous that they might be the last one to be chosen. It happened to *everyone* at one time or another. They'd all practised the dances for weeks at PE and knew them off by heart by now. Mr Irvine, the PE teacher announced the dances and controlled the music on the record player in the corner. It was great fun getting whirled around so fast by the boys. The faster the girls were whirled and the more everyone's feet stomped on the wooden floor, the more chance that the needle on the record would move and make the music jump all over the place! Everyone soon saw this and stomped and whirled all the harder to make it happen. And to see poor Mr Irvine scrambling to sort out the music again made everyone struggle not to laugh! Veronica and Elizabeth were there, but Shannon and Louisa stayed away from them and didn't let them spoil the chance to have great fun.

Towards the end of the evening, when everyone was grinning and exhausted with hours of dancing, Mr Irvine announced that there was to be a special 'treat'. A Primary Six pupil, Iain Marshall was going to play his trumpet along to a Christmas record that Mr Irvine had brought in. Everyone was a bit disappointed, as they were enjoying the dancing so much! They all expected to be forced to listen to a slow tooting along to

Silent Night! The record started and they heard sleigh bells. "Oh well, it sounds like Jingle Bells...again!" sighed Louisa to Shannon. But then a bouncy rhythm started. Everyone looked around at each other as the music went on, wondering exactly what kind of music old Mr Irvine had taken in. But then they heard trumpets blasting out from the record and Iain Marshall joined in as everyone's eyes opened wide with delight! This was no ordinary, boring Jingle Bells...this was the Glen Miller Orchestra! This was *their* music! No-one could believe that Mr Irvine listened to such modern music, or allowed it. But the proof was there as he closed his eyes, grinning and clicking his fingers to the rhythm as Iain blasted away on his trumpet beside him. The whole room went wild with dancing! At the end of the song Iain almost lifted the roof off with the tremendous noise of his trumpet and everyone stood, clapped and whistled, especially their classmate Norma, who jumped up and down clapping with delight more than anyone. Shannon and Louisa didn't know that she liked trumpet quite so much!

They grinned widely as they stood there exhausted and hot from dancing. "Come on Louisa" gasped Shannon "Let's go outside to the playground to cool down a while!" They pushed open the outside door, still giggling as they went out into the cool, dark, refreshing night air. They walked across the playground and over to the side wall of the lunch-hall and sat down, cooling off in the night breeze. They laughed, talking about the dance, until Louisa shivered. "Come on, let's go back inside Shannon" and they starts to walk back across the dark playground. But as they did they noticed two older girls coming towards them in the dark. Soon Shannon realised who these dark figures were - Veronica and Marjory! *Now* they were in *serious* trouble. "*Get them!*" snarled Veronica as Shannon and Louisa felt themselves being grabbed and hit to the ground. "Don't you *ever* try to mess us about again. I know what you did with that swing and I ended up soaking wet!" Louisa heard, as she felt herself being hit again in the back. Veronica turned to Shannon "And as for *you*, haven't you got any stupid stars to clean tonight?" she shouted. If only Veronica knew the *truth*. Shannon and Louisa said nothing, they were wet and sore on the ground and they had enough sense to know that if they said anything that they'd just end up getting hit more. Suddenly, some light spread out across the far side of the playground as the school door opened. Veronica and Marjory quickly turned and hurried off in the darkness, in case it was a teacher. They left the girls sore and crying on the wet ground. Shannon and Louisa helped each other up and when they got inside they saw that Louisa's tights were ripped and her knee was bleeding. Shannon had a cut elbow that stung. They got cleaned up in the toilets. "I've had enough!" said Shannon as they washed. "They've got to learn"! She turned to Louisa and noticed that her face was swollen with tears, like Mum's had been recently. Shannon *had* to sort them out once and for all. She couldn't beat them in a stupid fight and she knew that fighting was only for fools anyway. So she had to find another way, a *clever* way!

Grandad came and picked Shannon up a few minutes later. When he saw her he looked down at her face and saw her scratches and bruises. "What happened to you then Shannon?"
"Oh, I just fell when I was dancing Grandad". Of course, he knew that this wasn't true, but he didn't ask her again, knowing that she'd tell him in time. Before they got in to Mums Grandad stopped again to talk to Shannon. He leaned down and whispered to her "Now Shannon, you know that tomorrow's going to be a very sad day for your Mum at your Daddy's memorial service. You've got to be strong for her. You're so

lucky to actually know that your Daddy's doing fine, way up there. But your Mum must find it so *hard* to even *hope* that he's all right now Shannon. That's a *terrible* thing for her to have to feel! But *please, don't* tell her about Daddy and the stars, no matter how sad she gets. It's so important not to upset her more or risk having the stars ruined." Grandad looked down at her elbow, which was still bleeding a bit. "And you already know that when certain people don't believe you that they just laugh at you and pick on you. And I think that cut on your elbow knows it too, Shannon, eh?" He nodded down towards her scratched, bruised elbow "Do you understand?" She rubbed her elbow and nodded "Yes Grandad, I'll try my best" They wandered back into Mum's house, into the living room where Mum and Granny were sitting in front of the fireplace, with the only light being the fires' glow. It was surrounded by sympathy cards. She gave her Mum, Granny and Grandad a goodnight hug and kiss and then slowly walked upstairs to bed, feeling all her sore bits hurting on the way up. Mum didn't even seem to notice her bruised face. Once Shannon washed she went to her room, took down the sheet of black paper from the window and whispered up to the stars "Let me be strong tomorrow Daddy. God Bless!" She crept into bed and covered herself, slowly drifting off to sleep. Tomorrow was going to be a long day.

Chapter 18 – Dark Clouds

She woke up the next morning and decided to bring Mum up some tea and buttered toast on a tray to her bed. She put the tray down outside Mum's room and knocked on the door, but there was no answer. She nudged it open and quietly crept in with the tray and stood at the bottom of the bed. Mum was asleep. Her arms were wrapped around a pillow and the photo of Daddy was lying next to her on the bed. Shannon wished that she didn't have to wake Mum into such a terrible day, but she had to. She coughed, but Mum didn't wake, so she said "Morning Mum…." Mum slowly turned and opened her eyes "I've brought you some breakfast!" Mum slowly sat up in the bed and tried a quick smile to Shannon "That's so nice of you Shannon dear. Thank you." Shannon moved forward and placed the tray across her lap. Mum started to ask about the dance last night, but mostly she didn't know what to say today. She reached an arm over and gave Shannon a kiss and hug. "You go and get yourself washed and ready Shannon. And thank you again for the lovely breakfast!"

They both got themselves ready and soon there was a knock at the front door. Mum went and let Granny and Grandad in. There was lots of slow whispering, hugs and quiet breaks before the black taxi arrived outside the house. As they all walked out together Shannon saw the neighbours standing quietly and respectfully at their doors. Their neighbour, old Mr Ross bravely walked over the road from his garden and took Mum's arm to help her across the snowy pavement and into the taxi. As he did he whispered to her how sorry he was, before he walked down the road to join them at the church. He was Shannon's favourite neighbour, who often used to come across the road with his son, Alastair to listen to the football with Daddy on the radio. Soon their taxi pulled up at the church and they slowly walked in.

It was a long and strange day. Their priest, Father Davis was so good to Mum and offered her as many kind words as he could, but nothing could make her feel any better. As far as she was concerned all that was important was that she'd lost her beloved husband forever. Mum had asked that no flags were flown at the church, no uniforms were allowed to be worn and no mention to be made of him being a 'hero' by dying in a silly battle. Mum saw all these things as being very wrong – things which took her husband and her daughter's father away. And things which were senselessly still getting husbands, sons and fathers taken away from their loved ones every day, all around the world. It seemed to her that he'd been taken from them for nothing. Perhaps she thought it was just too difficult for most men to understand – or maybe they just didn't want to.

When the church service was finished they went to a local hotel for some sandwiches and tea and then decided to walk home. As they walked to Mum's with Granny and Grandad afterwards it was just starting to get dark. Shannon had been trying to be strong all day for Mum. Her throat was sore with trying to fight back her tears all day as she saw how absolutely lost, sad and hurt Mum was. Mum stopped on the way home to cry again on Grandad's shoulder. Shannon looked up, trying to stop her own tears from falling out of her eyes. As she did, the moon appeared from behind a cloud and she looked around at the whole sky. The first stars of the night were coming out. She knew that Dad was fine up there, safe and happy amongst the stars. And that Uncle Leo was up there on that glowing moon, possibly happily playing golf right now. And yet here was Mum down here, with her heart breaking. It all seemed so unfair.

Afterwards Granny and Grandad stayed at Mum's to keep her company. Shannon went up to bed, leaving them to talk downstairs. In her room she stared up at the stars again, whispering to Daddy how terrible it was that Mum couldn't believe and how unfair it all was that she couldn't tell her how everything was all right. As she whispered she stared at a star that she just knew was Daddy's.

Chapter 19 – Moving On

The next morning came and things went from bad to terrible. Shannon went into the living room and Mum wasn't there. Instead she found Mum's brother, Uncle Roy and their family doctor, Doctor McFadyen there. Uncle Roy was in his fishing jacket, so Shannon knew that he must have come up in a hurry from the river to get there. They saw her come in and looked a bit nervous. Uncle Roy walked over and gave her a hug as they both said good morning to her. She wondered what was going on. Doctor McFadyen spoke first - quietly and slowly "Shannon. Would you like to come and sit with us? Your Mother's asked me to tell you something. I'm afraid it's not good news Shannon." She sat down on the chair next to the window, confused and wondering what could be wrong now. She panicked for a few seconds, wondering if something had happened to Mum! But it wasn't that. Doctor McFadyen sat forward in his chair and looked at her, saying gently. "Before I go on Shannon, your Mum's safe and well…but it's your Grandad." Her heart jumped. "I'm afraid that he was taken into the hospital last night. He's not very well at all Shannon. Your Mum and your Granny are there with him just now. They asked if we could take you down to the hospital."
At that moment Shannon panicked. She forgot all about the fact that we actually just go to the stars – that we go on forever. Instead she just thought that she was losing Grandad forever now too! The tears of the last few days that she had kept in spilt out of her eyes in her panic.

They went down the road in Doctor McFadyen's car and soon their footsteps were clicking loudly down the polished corridors of the hospital, which had that strong 'hospital' chemical smell. They turned into a room full of hanging, light green curtains and saw Grandad. He was lying in a bed with his eyes shut, with Mum and Granny sitting by his side. They looked over at Shannon as she walked over to them and gave them a hug. Now *Granny's* face was puffy with tears too. Shannon hated to see that, but was happy to see Grandad's mouth moving. He was just asleep!

Mum stood up and took her out into the corridor, where they sat beside each other in two wooden chairs. She was shaking as she turned to Shannon and whispered "Shannon, I don't know how much you heard, but Grandad became very ill indeed last night. The doctors had a good look at him and….well…" Mum couldn't finish what she had to say and her face turned down towards the floor. But Shannon gently put her hand on Mum's and said "It's all right Mum, I know. Grandad's not going to be coming home. But Mum, he'll be all right when he goes, I just *know* it" Mum looked up, still shaking with sadness and gripped Shannon's hand tightly, before looking up at her and whispering "Oh Shannon, I'm so proud of you. You're so strong and full of hope!" They turned and hugged each other as Shannon wondered if she'd be even nearly as strong if she hadn't gone up to the stars and if she didn't know that we go on forever. Now she felt so incredibly lucky that she did. Mum told her that she was going to take Granny down to the hospital coffee shop for a little break, as she'd been up for most of the night and was exhausted. They went back into the room and Mum and Uncle Roy helped Granny up from her chair to take her out for a while, leaving Shannon to sit alone by Grandad's hospital bed.

She sat looking at Grandad sleep for a few quiet minutes, then looked around the room. Soon she heard a small, quiet chuckle of laughter come from the bed and turned her head to see him smiling and staring up at the ceiling above him. She stood up, looked down at him and held his hand "Hi Grandad!" she whispered. He slowly turned his head and looked at her. When he saw her, the smile grew on his face. He was so weak that he could hardly move or speak, but he whispered "Hi Shannon. Why on earth are you whispering, though, my wee girl? At least I've got an excuse!" She smiled back. He got straight to telling her "You know what's happening here Shannon? You *know* that I'll be moving on from this world very soon?" Shannon hated to hear this and said "Don't say that Grandad! You're going to get better." This made him just smile wider "Och Shannon. I can feel what's happening to me. I'm not daft, my dear, but why are you looking so scared? You *know* that I'll be fine. I'm as young *inside* this body as the day I was born. But this old wrinkly body itself's no use for a few rounds of boxing or a good footy match any more!" he smiled. He turned to face the ceiling and quietly laughed again. Shannon turned her head to see what he was looking at, but could see nothing up there except a thin layer of white paint. "Grandad – what are you looking at? What's so funny up there?" He turned his head to her "Och, it's just your Uncle Leo Shannon. He's waiting for me and just seeing that I'm all right to move on." He coughed and kept smiling at the ceiling "And he's telling me I'd better bring some spare golf balls because he's reminding me that I've lost most of his with bad shots!" Shannon couldn't see a thing. But she'd learnt now that just because she couldn't see Uncle Leo that it didn't mean that he wasn't there. Grandad turned to her again and whispered "Shannon, I've had such a *wonderful* time down here. I've done so many things, met so many people. And I'm surely *the* luckiest man there is. To have such a *wonderful* wife and family, to be given the chance to be a Starcarer, to *know* now that everything is going to be *absolutely* all right, that's *fantastic* to know Shannon! But now *you* know that too! Be strong Shannon and take special care of your Mummy

and Granny for me until I see them again. I trust you to do that, my girl."
She smiled at him and nodded, but said "But I'll *miss* you Grandad!" He
whispered "Come here Shannon." She hugged him gently as he stroked
her hair and he said "That's all right. It's natural to miss people. But you
should know now that you can't really miss *me*, because *I'll always* be
with you, no matter what - just like your Daddy is. You'll miss your eyes
seeing me and your ears hearing me down here. But you know now,
that's not really who *I* am! These bodies that we live in are important, but
they're only for a short time. Do you understand?" She stood up and
nodded again.

"And Shannon, it's *your* job now to care for the stars. The bike's yours
now. I saw Uncle Tuppence and Mr Morran this morning and they'll help
you out, so don't worry about that." He reached out to the bedside table
and handed her two keys, telling her that they were the keys to open up
the church and the back door of the museum. He reminded her that the
ladder was round the back of the church. And he asked her to see Uncle
Tuppence soon so that he could tell her how the radio worked in the
community centre – so that she'd know which stars needed to be visited
and when.

She was a bit scared to be left in charge of doing something so important,
but said to Grandad "No problem Grandad, it'll be fine." He turned his
head to look and smile at the ceiling again. She knew that he was truly
seeing Leo up there, but she just sat and stared at his face as he smiled
upwards, looking so peaceful and happy.

After a few silent minutes he turned his smiling head to look at her again
and gently squeezed her hand "Now Shannon. It's time to go. There's no
point in you hanging around here. Go off for a long walk down on that

wonderful beach for me. I'll tell your Mum that I asked you to go there."
She was sad when he said this, but soon knew that it made sense. She
was so lucky not to have to walk out of the room thinking that this was the
last time she'd see him - she *knew* better. She gently leant over the bed
and kissed him, then smiled and said "Goodbye Grandad". He smiled at
her comment and said "Good grief Shannon, what use is that word
'*Goodbye*'? I've *never* understood that word. Do you know that your
Uncle Leo had a pal called Hugh McKenzie. He worked over in North
America for a wee while and he told me that the Cree Indians don't have
a word for 'Goodbye'! Now hearing that I always thought that they must
be *really* clever and wonderful people. So, Shannon....what *does* make
sense is '*See you later*!" he winked. "All right Grandad......see you later."
She let his hand go and slowly walked out. As she turned she saw him
staring up at the ceiling again, smiling as widely as he ever had!

She wandered out of the hospital and down to the sea. She had the
whole beach to herself. As she walked along the sand she found it
strange and maybe felt a bit guilty that she wasn't feeling very sad right
now. She was happy for Grandad, knowing that he was going to be safe
and fine – and more 'full of life' than he had ever been. As she often did
on the beach, she met Sam, a neighbour's dog there and spent hours
walking along the sand with him. She threw him sticks to chase and
skimmed flat stones across the low waves that he'd chase into the cold
water and take back to her. Sam was such a wonderful friend!

The sky started to turn to a darker blue and she decided to walk back
towards home. The moon appeared and she started to shout out to Leo
up there that Grandad would be with him soon. As she walked, she drew
huge pictures on the sand with a piece of driftwood - pictures of stars, of

a winged bike, of men playing golf on the moon. And just before she left the beach she wrote in huge letters "See You Later Grandad!" As soon as she finished, Sam suddenly started wagging his tail excitedly and barking up at the sky. He was looking straight up at the first star of the night, twinkling so brightly. Shannon knew that Grandad had moved on, *right* then. She threw the stick into the salty water and the waves gently pulled it out to sea. She stood and stared smiling at that star for a while, before she and Sam turned around and walked up the road towards home.

Chapter 20 – An Icy Trip

Shannon woke up the next morning. It was Christmas Eve. She wandered downstairs and found Mum and Granny talking in the living room in front of the fire. They still sounded so sad and all that they talked about was arrangements for Grandad's memorial service in a few days time. There were no decorations this year. There would be no radio on to hear the Christmas carols, no preparing things for Christmas lunch tomorrow, no neighbours coming round to join the family for a Christmas party. For poor Mum and Granny it must have seemed right now that Christmas and hope were dead. Last night when Shannon got home there wasn't much talking at all – just Mum telling her that Grandad had 'gone'. What could Shannon possibly say or do that morning to make things better? She got dressed, grabbed a quick snack of bread and jam, said that she was going round to Louisa's and then wandered out onto the frosty pavement.

She knocked on Louisa's door. Her Mum opened it. She was such a cheery lady and always full of fun. But today was different. She just stood there with her mouth open, looking shocked to see Shannon. She bent down and touched her shoulder, saying "I'm so sorry to hear the news Shannon dear. Are you all right?" Shannon just nodded. "Well you give your family my love Shannon. And if there's anything I can do, just ask." Shannon nodded again "Thank you Mrs McHardy". Louisa's Mum carried on "Right. You'll be wanting to see Louisa. Come on in out of the cold" she said, as Shannon followed her into the hall. "Just go upstairs Shannon". She knocked on Louisa's door and slowly pushed it open, finding her sitting on her bed reading a comic. She looked up at Shannon and looked even more shocked to see her than her Mum was! But Shannon had enough of people being sad, or not knowing what to say and said "Good grief Louisa, I'm here to play, not to cry! I'm fine, now let's go!." Soon they were playing and laughing like nothing bad had happened at all. Mrs McHardy came up with some lemonade and biscuits and asked them if they'd seen "the snow out there". They jumped up on Louisa's bed to look outside and they could hardly see the house across the road through the slow, thick snowflakes that were floating down. Louisa's Mum said that it was all right for them to go outside. They didn't wait to be asked!

They rushed out onto the squeaky blanket of white outside, the snowflakes covering their coats in seconds! They laughed as they ran round the corner towards where the road went down the hill, catching snowflakes on their tongues and hurling snowballs at each other on the way. They started to build an ice-slide down the pavement. Over and over again they ran and slid forward as far as they could, until the slide slowly grew longer and more slippery, then rubbed the snow hard with the bottom of their shoes, to make it as slippery and icy as possible! Pretty soon they had a wonderful, shining ice-slide that went all the way down the pavement, right to the bottom of the hill. The only tricky bit was managing to stop at the bottom! Every race they had down the hill was filled with screams of laughter. They saw nice old Mr Ross, from across the road appear round the corner at the bottom of the hill, weighed down with a shopping bag in each hand. They watched him struggle slowly up the snowy pavement, next to their icy slide! They called out to him to take care as they started to walk down the hill to help him out. Unfortunately Mr Ross' hearing wasn't so good and about half way up the hill he stepped onto the slide and immediately started to slip about, his legs flying around as he tried to stay on his feet and his shopping bags flapping about in the air around him! Somehow he didn't fall down and a few seconds later he managed to get his feet steady, gasping with relief. But then panic spread across his face ….as he started to slip slowly backwards! The girls started to run down the hill to make sure that he was all right, but as they got closer he was now travelling backwards down the icy slide at running speed, his shopping bags waving in the air, like two windmills in a storm! They felt terrible and ran after him as he got faster and faster, hoping that he wouldn't get hurt! But he didn't stop and the girls knew what would come next. Their icy slide finished and Mr Ross flipped over, landing on his back in a pile of snow, with tins and vegetables from his bags spinning off in all directions across the snow around him. The girls were absolutely horrified!

Their running slowed down as they got close to Mr Ross. They bent down to help him sit up. They were *so* happy that he didn't look as though he was hurt at all – because he was such a nice man. But they thought that even he would be angry and that they'd be in serious trouble for this. But to their surprise he just sat up, eyes wide open, pink faced, covered in snow, hair sticking up and looking amazed at each of them…..and then he burst into laughter! Shannon and Louisa looked at each other, amazed at this! They were even more amazed by what he said next, between his laughs. "Fantastic!" he said "That's the best fun I've had in years!" The girls looked at each other again and then at Mr Ross lying back in the snow and laughing and that started them off laughing too! The girls walked around picking up his groceries and putting them back into the bags, all three of them still laughing out loud! They helped Mr Ross up the hill with his bags, but he surprised them when he asked to stop at the top – because he wanted another go on the slide! The girls were amazed as they saw this nice old man sliding and screaming his way down the hill on ice and thought that it was both hilarious and fantastic at the same time! And Shannon grinned as she remembered Grandad being the same when they cycled down that hill near Brackla on his bike. They carried the bags to Mrs Ross' front gate with him and he went into his house with the last of his Christmas groceries, still smiling like a young boy!

It was a fantastic break for Shannon after the last couple of days. Being with Louisa had really cheered her up. They went back to Louisa's house and her Mum made them a nice cup of cocoa and some iced biscuits. Their frozen hands were stinging against the edges of the hot mugs. But it tasted so good and warming that they didn't care! Mrs McHardy was puzzled as to why they were giggling so much as they drank and ate. But the girls weren't exactly going to tell her what happened on the hill in case they got in trouble!

Shannon walked back round to her house. Mum and Granny were chatting in the front room and Shannon could see that they'd both been crying again. After such a fun day it was *horrible* to come back into such sadness. They didn't mention going to church for the Christmas celebrations at midnight. So Shannon took it that they weren't going. Tomorrow it was Christmas Day and it looked like being such a miserable one, but she didn't want to be selfish. She hugged and kissed them and went to bed.

It was Christmas morning. Shannon woke up and looked down at the bottom of the bed. At least Santa hadn't forgotten her. One of Daddy's long woollen socks was stuffed at the bottom of her bed. She sat up and opened it. There were lots of nuts, some oranges, a small dolly, some sweets and some pencils for school. She smiled as she looked at the presents scattered across her bed. Outside there was still plenty of snow around, so it should be another fun day for sliding or sledging with Louisa. Shannon went through to Mum's room, but she wasn't there. She wandered down the stairs, then through to the living room, where she noticed that Santa had left her a skipping rope and a lovely, thick Icelandic jumper on the sofa. *Just* what she'd asked for! She wandered across the room, excited about her new jumper. But as she did she turned and noticed that Granny was hugging Mum in the corner and that they were both crying again. Shannon felt bad for them, but she now felt angry too. This was Christmas! It just wasn't *fair* that they were so sad. And it wasn't fair that everyone's Christmas was being ruined!

The day was long and quiet. Even during Christmas lunch hardly a word was said. The only real sound of any kind was of the seconds ticking away on the clock above the fireplace. Although Mum *did* put on the radio for a little while, Shannon *knew* that Daddy and Grandad would *hate* everyone to be sad on Christmas Day, just 'because of' them. For the first Christmas ever they never went to church. They just didn't feel up to it. Shannon really wanted to go round to play with Louisa, but decided that it was right that she should spend all day with Mum and Granny today.

It started to grow dark and Shannon stared out of the living room window at the dark blue sky above, which was starting to fill with twinkling stars. Mum and Granny went through to the kitchen to make some tea and Shannon took the chance to look up at the sky and whisper a "Happy Christmas" to Daddy and Grandad up there. Thinking of them up there made her smile for the first time that Christmas Day. But when she turned round she saw Granny sitting forward in her chair. She had her hands over her face and Shannon could see her shoulders shaking. She *knew* that Granny was crying, but trying to do it secretly, without Shannon hearing. Shannon's heart sank again, but she was also absolutely *fed up* of all of this sadness! She knew very well what Grandad and Daddy had told her about not saying anything about the bike and about meeting Dad and caring for the stars. But she'd had *enough* of tears and sadness. This was it! She just *had* to tell them, she wanted to *show* them!

Mum walked back into the room from the kitchen and put her arm around Granny. Shannon took a deep breath and looked out of the window at the sky, whispering "Sorry Grandad, I've got to…!" and then walked across the room to them. Granny saw her coming and wiped her tears, saying "Sorry about my crying Shannon….I didn't want to upset you!" Shannon just stood and shook her head, saying "You don't need to say sorry Granny. I know that you're missing Grandad. But Granny, I also know what can make you and Mum happy and I need you to believe what I'm about to tell you". Granny could see that she was serious. "All right Shannon." said Granny "Sit yourself down and let's talk then, eh?" She sat and Mum said "All right then Shannon…you wanted to tell us something". Shannon gulped, nervous about telling them – about what they'd think. "Well, it's like this" started Shannon "you remember that Grandad used to tell me about going up to care for the stars?" she asked. Mum smiled "Yes Shannon, I do and those stories were *really* nice! Your Grandad was a lovely story-teller." she smiled. Shannon looked at both of them and carefully said "But Mum…it *isn't* just a story….it's *true*!" Mum nodded and said "Shannon, it's so nice that you believe his stories and if you want to believe them, we're fine with that!" But Shannon was determined to say more, no matter how stupid it might sound to them. She shook her head. "*No* Mum, I'm sorry, but you *don't* understand. I went up to the stars with him....on his bike! I can take *you* up there on it today!" Mum's face turned pale at hearing this and Shannon saw that she was getting angry too.

Shannon turned to Granny and said "Come on Granny. *Please* come with me, It'll cheer you up!" As Granny heard this her eyes closed and her tears started to flow as she turned her head down to hide them. Mum looked over at Shannon and angrily started to shout at her "Shannon, *enough* of your stories! Are you trying to make things worse by saying such *ridiculous* things at a time like this? *Why* are you saying this? Shannon...your Daddy and Grandad are *gone*! Do you *understand*? *Forever*! *That's* what's important now, *not* silly stories! Do you *hear* me? *Stop* it now!" Shannon had never seen Mum so furious before! She ran out of the room, saying "Why can't you just *believe* me? Just give me a chance to show you that it's all *true*! I just wanted to cheer you up." She left them in the room and ran out into the dark blue snowy garden and the cold Christmas night air. She was angry and sad, but didn't know what to do. She had to prove it to them, but how? She had just about decided to give up when she had an idea.

She ran inside and up the stairs to her room. She dived onto the floor and felt under the wardrobe, before bringing out the small, flowery metal box of stardust that Grandad had given her. She walked down into the living room with it. Mum stared at her, still angry and Shannon knew that it would take a lot to get them to believe anything right now. And even more to hopefully come down to the museum and up to the stars with her! She held out her hand to show them the box and said "Grandad gave me this lovely wee box not long ago" Granny looked at it in her hand and said "That's a *lovely* present Shannon. Such beautiful flowers on it too. Your Grandad loved you *so* much." But Shannon shook her head, saying "No

Granny, it's not just that he "*loved*" me…he *loves* me – *and* you! And you're right Granny, this *is* a beautiful box, but it's what's *inside* that's the important thing! *That* is what makes us fly! Granny…you *have* to believe that you'll see Grandad again one day, t*oday* if you like!" Granny looked straight at her and whispered "I *know* that you mean well Shannon. I know what I *should* believe and what I hear every time that I go to church. But you have to understand that right now I find that so *hard* to believe, my dear."

Shannon then heard Mum shouting at her again "Now you *stop* that Shannon! Can't you see that you're upsetting Granny with all of this *nonsense*?" But Shannon couldn't stop now. She put the small box in Granny's hand and said "*Please* Granny, *trust* me. Just open the box - *please*." Granny looked down at the box and her old hands slowly fiddled with it until the lid clicked open. As she opened its tiny lid, her face turned from dark and full of sadness and tears, to being full of surprise and glowing a fantastic gold! Granny and Mum gasped. They had never seen a colour like this anywhere, ever before! Mum turned to Shannon, whispering "*What* is that stuff in there Shannon?" Shannon replied "It's stardust Mum, *real* stardust! You *have* to believe me!" Shannon expected Mum to laugh when she said it was stardust, but Mum said nothing. She must have realised that it was something *very* special indeed! Shannon continued "Please, come with me and I'll take you up to the stars tonight if you want to see for yourself!"
Mum turned to her with a confused look on her face. Shannon could see that Mum didn't yet believe her and that she just didn't really understand what she was trying to say. It was all too incredible a story for her.
"*Please* Mum, trust me. I promise you *in Daddy's name* that I'm not lying!"
Mum stopped and stared deep into Shannon's eyes for saying this. She

hoped that Shannon wouldn't promise on something as special to her as Daddy, unless she meant it and to Shannon's utter amazement Mum said "All right Shannon, we'll come with you. Whatever that stuff is in this box, it's *truly* beautiful. I don't know what you're up to, but we'll come with you anyway darling, all right?" Shannon walked through to the hall, delighted and came back in with their coats, her heart racing. "Well, what are we waiting for?" she asked. As Mum put on her coat she looked straight at her and said with a serious looking face "Look Shannon. It's freezing out there and getting dark. If you're just saying this to cheer me and Granny up, just say now and we'll understand. It's your last chance!" But Shannon hugged her and looked up at her face, saying "Mum, please just try to believe!"

They all got on their coats and walked along the snowy path and down through the evening towards the church, where a very special pot of fresh stardust was waiting for them, high above the altar.

Chapter 21 - Hoping

Mum and Granny breathed out icy clouds around them as they walked through the thick snow behind Shannon, wondering what on earth they were doing following her. Were they being silly? Possibly. But there was *something* in Shannon's words, *something* in the wonderful colour of that glowing dust in the small tin that made them follow – *just* in case! They walked silently down the road. It was a sparkly winter's evening and the streets were practically empty. Everyone else would be inside happily full up with Christmas cake and playing with their presents. Soon they were walking by the church and were surprised when Shannon turned and opened the squeaky metal gate and walked in. Mum and Granny stood outside the it, asking her "*What are you doing*?" But Shannon reached into her coat and took out Grandad's key, winking as she held it up to show them. Granny and Mum looked at each other, wondering what was going on and *why* she had a church key!

Shannon opened the door and said, "Could you wait in there for me, please? I've got to get something." They crept in and sat in near darkness in their usual row of seats in the church and started to pray for Daddy and Grandad. The small lamp down at the front of the church made its small, red glow. But their prayers were suddenly stopped by a loud bang from the door behind them. They turned round to see the front end of a ladder coming in through the door. Mum stood up and walked towards it and as she did so, she saw Shannon appear, pushing it inside. Mum looked at her, puzzled "What on Earth is going on Shannon?" she asked, as she grabbed an end of the ladder. Shannon replied "Oh, you'll soon find out Mum! Could you please help me take it down towards the altar?" They carried the ladder down through the church, sometimes knocking it on the rows of church seats, the bangs echoing off the church walls around them. Granny followed them up the steps and on to the altar. Shannon stopped under the baldequino (her 'Baldy Queen' balcony') and asked Mum to help her stand the ladder high up against the edge of it. Mum looked shocked "We can't do *that* Shannon! I mean…why on *Earth* do you want to go up there?" Shannon smiled in the red glow of the lamp "Just hold the ladder steady as I go up, please Mum. I'll be fine." Together they raised the ladder up, leaning it against the baldequino. Mum held it at the bottom as Shannon climbed. She and Granny looked at each other as if to say "What on Earth are we *doing* here?" But their eyes soon opened wide as they turned and saw a beautiful ray of golden light shine from the picture at the back of the church, across to the big, stained-glass window and then rush down the church towards Shannon, above them! They gasped and Mum whispered up to her "Shannon! What's that *beautiful* light?" as it slowly disappeared. Shannon just giggled and said "Mum, I'll tell you later, honest!" Mum steadied the ladder as Shannon climbed back down with Grandad's pot of fresh stardust tucked safely into her coat pocket.

Soon they left the church and Shannon asked them to follow her further down the road, along the snowy, twinkling pavements. They followed on, then up the side road to the museum. Shannon walked around the back – a shadow in the moonlight. She took another key out from her coat and put it into the lock at the back door. Mum was shocked! "Shannon, what are you doing *now*?" she slowly asked. Looking around in panic, in case someone was watching them. But Shannon just smiled as she clicked the key in the wooden door and slowly swung it open.

It was dark inside, but Shannon could see the shadow of the bike in there, so she asked Mum and Granny to be careful as they came in. Shannon shut the door behind them. Granny and Mum stood there in the dark as Shannon felt about for a light-switch for a few seconds. Mum's voice sounded scared in the dark "Shannon...right, this *isn't* funny! We're going home, come on Granny!" Shannon heard Mum's hands feeling at the door for the handle, but she found the light switch and the shed lit up. Shannon looked across at Mum and Granny who suddenly stood staring at the strange *'thing'* in front of them, their mouths wide open in shock! But then Granny did something that Shannon *definitely* didn't expect at all! She burst into laughter and pointed at the winged bike, as Mum just kept staring at it. "It's your Grandad's bike Shannon. And look, he went and made some wings for it! Fantastic!" laughed Granny. "Come on Shannon, I never knew about this. Did he do that for a laugh? Did he do it for a Christmas pantomime or something?" It was the first time that Shannon had seen Granny smile for a couple of days, so she was glad, but a bit confused by Granny's reaction and she slowly answered. "No Granny. It's *not* for a pantomime...it really *does* fly!" Granny laughed more, saying "Oh Shannon. I'll tell you what, your Grandad was a brilliant story-teller and you *certainly* got that from him, my dear!" She wandered around the bike and across to Shannon and kissed her forehead, saying gently "Oh *thank you* Shannon, seeing this cheered me up! It was worth the walk through the snow my dear!"

Then Shannon looked over at Mum though, who did *not* look happy at all! "You both still don't believe me at all, do you?" said Shannon "You think that this is just an old, ordinary bike that someone's put some made-up feathers onto for some kind of Christmas show and that I'm just making it all up!" Mum looked really angry now and she jerked her arms around as she said "No Shannon! Of *course* we don't believe you - *look* at it! It's just an old *bike*! We walked your Granny here through a cold, snowy night. We sneaked into the church and now into here, just to see some rusty old bike with some home-made feathers strapped onto it and *you* expect us to believe that it *flies? Come on* my girl, we're going home…*now*!" she shouted, as she reached for the door handle.

Shannon knew that she meant it and shook her head, resting her hand on the box-trailer, *so* disappointed that it seemed like they'd *never* believe. Mum opened the door as Granny tapped Shannon on the shoulder and followed out. But Shannon took one last chance and shouted "*Mum!*" She turned back, *furious* that Shannon had shouted at her, *especially* after all this! But Shannon said quietly "I'm sorry Mum, but I *have* to say this. Tonight I promised you in my *Daddy's name* that this bike can take us to the stars, do you remember?" Mum's face changed from angry to being sorry almost instantly. Shannon carried on, calmly saying "Mum I *know* that you love me and Daddy. But the strange thing is that you can't *prove* that you love him, can you? We can't see our love or touch it - we all just *know* it! I *promise* you again in Dad's *and* Grandad's names that this "rusty old" bike can take us all up to the stars! If you just *believe* enough, give me a chance and come with me tonight, I'll *prove* to you that we *can* fly to those wonderful stars up there!" Mum's eyes were full of tears at hearing this and all she could do was nod. She opened the wooden doors, grabbed the handlebars and slowly started to push the bike out onto the park. Shannon helped her by pushing the back of the box-trailer, smiling widely. They closed the doors behind them and Shannon walked over the snow to Mum and hugged her, saying "Thank you for giving me a chance Mum!" As they hugged each other Shannon looked out over the wide, snow-blanketed park around them where she and Grandad had taken-off into the air from before. She thought of her pal Louisa and

153

wished that she was here to come up to the stars with them too. But *that* just gave her a *brilliant* idea!

She giggled to herself about what she was thinking and said to Mum and Granny "Before we go, I've got one last thing to do! Instead of just taking the bike and trailer into this snowy field, can you help me take it down the road, towards Bunker's Brae?" Mum asked her why. Shannon replied "Oh, there's just something that I want to do down there with this bike." "Oh-oh! That sounds risky to me Shannon!" said Granny "Do you know that a long time ago a man used to try and fly off that hill with home-made flying machines and he always ended up crashing!" Shannon smiled at her "Yes Granny. Grandad told me - but apparently the man didn't *always* crash!" she said. When Mum heard this she turned to look at Shannon, who just smiled and said "Trust me Mum, I'm not going to do anything daft!" They pushed the winged bike and trailer down the path and along the road towards Bunker's Brae, the dark blue twinkling sky above them. Shannon grinned all the way, because she'd finally convinced Granny and Mum to come with her.

Soon they were getting close to the steep hill of Bunker's Brae -and going past nasty Veronica's big, grand house. Shannon asked Mum and Granny to walk along to the top of the hill and wait for her on the bench there, as she "just *had* to do something!" They were a bit puzzled, but then they were puzzled a lot that night anyway, so they walked along to the top of the steep hill to wait. Shannon opened the gate to Veronica's garden, walked along the path and up the steps to the front of the grand house. She knocked the big round door-knocker on the heavy wooden door and heard someone coming from inside. She should be scared, but she knew *exactly* what she was doing. She looked around at the sky and sea behind her, before she turned back around smiling as the door was opened and lit up the doorstep. A tall lady stood looked down at her and Shannon said "Hello, I'm sorry to bother you on Christmas Day, but is Veronica there please?" The lady smiled back at her, saying "That's all right, I'll just get her" as she disappeared into the house. Shannon thought that the woman *can't* be Veronica's Mum – she was *far* too nice! A few seconds later Veronica appeared at the door. When she saw Shannon there she scrunched up her nose in snobbish disgust! "Oh my goodness, what do you think *you're* doing here Shannon?" Shannon just smiled up at her "Oh, I just thought that I'd come by to show you my Christmas present." Veronica cackled like a witch, saying "And do you *really* think that I'd be interested in any poor little present that *you* got? I didn't think that your family could *afford* presents!" This hurt, but Shannon didn't show it. Instead she just smiled and replied "Actually I got a lovely bike! There it is, parked on the grass over there. It's *very* special!" Shannon moved to one side and pointed as Veronica stared across the road, before she burst into more screeching laughter! But this didn't stop Shannon, who said "*And* it can fly! I told you before that my Grandad cared for the stars – and now it's my turn to do it. Come with me and I'll show you it flying!" With that Veronica laughed even louder. Veronica's Mum came to the door again, wondering what all of the laughter was about and asked "Would you like to invite your friend in Veronica? It's very cold out here?" Veronica turned and laughed sarcastically "Did you say '*friend*' Mum?" She turned to look at Shannon again with an evil look on her face, saying "No Mum, I'm just going out for a little while. This '*friend*' of mine is going to show me her new, *wonderful* Christmas present!" Veronica's Mum looked confused, but wished Shannon a Happy Christmas and went back inside as Veronica grabbed her coat. She almost bounced down the path with Shannon, still laughing. She couldn't *wait* to make more fun of her and her bike!

As the gate swung shut behind them, Veronica said nastily "Right then! Let's see your rusty, ancient, useless, *poor* Christmas present then eh?" Shannon walked over to the bike and put her hand on the handlebar, saying proudly "Here it is!" That just started Veronica laughing even more. She stood there pointing at the old bike, tears of laughter running down her face. Veronica was enjoying every *second* of this and *loving* just how much she thought it would hurt Shannon. "You mean to tell me that this rusty old thing *really is* your *Christmas present* Shannon? Isn't this just your Grandad's shaky old bike?" She held the tip of a wing between her fingers, as if it was something absolutely disgusting, saying "And what fool made these *pathetic* old wings and attached them to the bike? And apparently it *flies*? Your really *are* a stupid little girl Shannon!"

Shannon was hurt by many things that Veronica was saying, but she kept calm inside, hoping that she'd soon be able to get her own back on this horrible, snobby girl! Shannon spoke up, louder than Veronica's laughter and pointed towards Bunker's Brae, saying "Veronica. Do you know that a long time ago a man ran off Bunker's Brae in a homemade flying machine and that he managed to fly into the sky from it?" Veronica put her finger to her mouth, cheekily making it look as though she was thinking about what Shannon said "Oh yes Shannon, I seem to remember hearing about an old *fool* who tried that years ago. But I think that maybe you got the story about that man a bit *wrong*! You see, the truth is that he crashed *every* time he tried and everyone just pointed and *laughed* at him!" Veronica started to walk around the bike, pointing and cackling at it even more. Shannon just stood there, not saying a word. She had a plan to get her own back on Veronica by flying off Bunker's Brae on the bike and proving her wrong, but as Veronica nastily laughed her way around the bike Shannon suddenly got scared! She started to feel sick, wondering if she'd made a *huge* mistake! What if the bike can only fly from the field behind the museum? Maybe it was a special field! Grandad never said. She might cycle the bike off Bunker's Brae and crash at bottom of the hill too! She'd possibly get very hurt and Veronica would make her life at school *terrible*. She'd tell all of her friends and Shannon would end up getting laughed at for years! But she knew it was too late to turn back now and looked up at the night sky, asking Grandad to help her down here. She just *had* to make the bike fly!

With her heart pounding she turned around to Veronica and said "Look, I've told you that this bike can fly. Let's go along to Bunker's Brae and I'll *prove* it to you, I'll fly it off the hill into the sky!" Veronica just stood staring at Shannon, her eyes wide open in surprise. She couldn't believe what Shannon was saying. She burst into that horrid laughter again as Shannon started to push the bike along the path to Bunker's Brae. Veronica followed, shouting "Fantastic! I can't *wait* to see you crashing your stupid old bike into the bottom of the hill and then telling everybody about it when we get back to school!" Shannon was terrified to hear her say that and she started to find it hard to believe that this was going to work. She pushed the bike along, gulping as Bunker's Brae got closer and closer and her heart thumped faster with every step she took.

She could see Mum and Granny sitting on the bench at the top of the hill ahead and could hear Veronica still laughing horribly behind her. It was *so* embarrassing! Mum stood up and asked Shannon if she was all right, which stopped Veronica laughing and she stood back on the path. She could hardly *wait* to see Shannon crashing! Shannon just nodded to show Mum that she was all right. She stopped the bike back a bit from the top of the hill. The dark, sparkling sky and moon shone above and the sea twinkled in the distance in front of her. She walked over and stood at the edge of the hill and looked down. Its' steepness was covered in shiny, icy, hard tracks where people had been sledging all day. If this didn't work, she was going to get *seriously* hurt! She turned and walked back to the bike and climbed onto the seat, putting on her goggles. Mum stood up, saying "Shannon! What do you think you're doing? This is *stupid*! You're *not* going to go crashing down Bunker's Brae on that thing!" Shannon looked back at her and Granny and said "I hope that you're right Mum. I don't want to go down there either...I want to *fly*!" With that Veronica started to laugh again, but Mum turned to Veronica and shouted "Don't you *dare* laugh at my Daughter, you *nasty* girl!" Veronica stopped and faced the ground, but still had an evil smile on her face. Shannon looked forward into the sky again. *Now* was the time! She stood up on the pedals and Mum started to march towards her, saying "Don't be silly Shannon!" As she did Veronica ran over the snow to the edge of the hill – she just *had* to get the best view of Shannon crashing! Imagine the fun of telling everyone at school!

Shannon quickly reached into her jacket and dipped her fingertip into the stardust tin. She quickly wiped some on the tip of each wing, put the tin back in her coat pocket and pushed down on the pedals with all her might. The bike started to move slowly forwards, picking up speed with each push of the pedals over the packed snow, towards the top of the hill. She heard Mum turn and scream "Shannon!" behind her and she saw Veronica grinning at the hilltops edge ahead, very happily waiting for her to fall and get hurt – but she kept pedalling anyway! Shannon looked up at the moon in hope and closed her eyes tight, expecting a painful fall and crash. She felt the edge of the hill come and the bike dive downwards! She gasped as her eyes opened and gripped the handlebars *so* tightly, seeing the hard ground rushing towards her! She waited for the huge crash and the pain...........!

Chapter 22 – Believing

But there was no crash...and there was no pain! Instead there was a
beautiful flash of white light from the wings as they suddenly flapped and
swooped her up into the night sky, her hair blowing back behind her in
the wind! She gasped with delight and looked back below her to see
Veronica standing there, staring up at her! Granny and Mum were
jumping up and down with joy! It *worked*! She thought of going back down
to get Mum and Granny and immediately the bike gently turned and
glided back down towards them. As she came in to land at the top of the
hill she thought of that man who flew off there all of those years ago; and
of how *delighted* he would be to see her right now.

Mum and Granny were amazed! They stared as they rushed over and
stopped next to the glowing bike. It was *incredible*! Mum grabbed
Shannon and hugged her "Oh Shannon, you were *right*! And Grandad
was right!" As they hugged Shannon looked around and asked where
Veronica had gone, but then saw her running back towards her house,
screaming "Daaaad!" Shannon panicked! She couldn't let *anyone* else
know about this, e*specially* someone like Veronica! She jumped off the
bike and quickly opened the trailer box, saying to Mum and Granny
"Quickly, jump in!" They looked into the dark, dusty box and weren't too
happy about doing that, but they changed their mind when they saw the
panicky look on Shannon's face as she begged them "*Please*! *Trust* me!"
Mum nodded and helped Granny climb in and then quickly jumped in
behind her, as Shannon leapt back on the bike seat and rubbed a bit
more stardust on the wing tips. The wings started to flap again, as Mum
held onto Granny in the back. Shannon could see Veronica was now

running up her garden path in the distance and shouted over her shoulder "Hold on!" to Mum and Granny. The bike pushed forwards, getting faster across the snowy hilltop and then soared up into the night sky. As they flew up Shannon turned around to check on Mum and Granny, shouting "Are you alright back there?" But they couldn't speak. They just nodded in amazement as they looked all around themselves at the sparkling, snowy ground and sea below them as they raced upwards into that twinkling sky. Their town looked *fantastic* from up here! They excitedly pointed out where the church was, their houses, the harbour as they climbed further and further upwards.

Down below Veronica's Dad was staring at her and shaking his head as she pulled at his jumper in their house, screaming for him to come outside and see a glowing, flying bike! Her family had just finished Christmas dinner and he was full-up. The last thing that he wanted right now was to go outside into the cold, but Veronica kept screaming and so he came outside to see what on Earth all her fuss was about. She pointed up at the sky over the sea and she shouted out "There it is!" as a tiny shadow moved across the sky in front of them. He just sighed and shook his head, saying "It's just another aeroplane Veronica". She screamed again that it was a flying bike. But he got fed up of her shouting and ordered her to get back inside and stop being so silly! She stomped in the door past him, annoyed that he didn't believe her. As she walked past, he said "Do you *really* expect anyone to believe such a ridiculous story Veronica? I'll bet if you told anyone at school something as ridiculous as that you'd end up getting *bullied for speaking such rubbish!*" She turned and stared angrily at him, before running up the stairs to her room to sulk! He shook his head and went back through to relax in front of the fire.

Meanwhile up in the sky there were two amazed, proud women and a happy little girl flying up towards the stars! Mum and Granny stared all around at the fantastic views below and soon they were flying through and above the misty clouds, which spread out like a fluffy blanket below them. They suddenly felt very cold and cuddled into each other for warmth. Shannon shouted over her shoulder to them "Very soon you'll find it harder to breath. But don't worry, it's only for a few seconds and it'll be fine; and we'll be warmer too, you're safe." Almost as soon as Shannon said this they did indeed feel it harder to breath. But then they saw Shannon flick her finger into the air around them, which sparkled that fantastic gold as the wings changed to the same wonderful colour. It was suddenly so warm and quiet as the Earth grew smaller and smaller behind them.

In the warm quiet of space Mum and Granny got their first chance since going up in the air to just sit back and enjoy the incredible views all around them! Their heads were buzzing with the excitement of it all. They could hardly believe how *incredible* all of this was! Shannon turned as she heard Granny saying "We're *so* proud of you Shannon, you showed us that it was all true. We're so sorry that we didn't believe you." Shannon smiled and turned as she felt a hand resting warmly on her shoulder, to see Mum's face smiling so proudly at her. Mum looked around at the twinkling space all around them and proudly said to Shannon "So now I know it's true, that Grandad and now *you* go to the stars. And here you are – taking us to them tonight! There are just so many stars up here though Shannon! How can you possibly know which one to go to?" Shannon laughed, remembering that she thought the same not long ago when she came up with Grandad and said "Mum, you just enjoy the view and think of whatever you want to and I'm sure that we'll just end up going to the most important star in the sky that there is for us, trust me!" After what she'd seen tonight, Mum knew very well to trust what she said. So she tapped Shannon's shoulder and sat back down next to Granny again. As the glowing wings gently flapped Mum and Granny just sat with their feet facing backwards, watching the Earth slowly shrinking behind them.

Just like Shannon did before, Mum looked back down at the Earth, found where France was and stared at it. She thought about her husband. Down there was where he last breathed. Where she believed he was taken away from them forever by a pointless war. She wished that he could be with them now, up in this wonderful place. He'd be *so* happy and proud. She found out that even in such a wonderful, happy place, she actually hurt inside too, because the man that she loved more than words couldn't be here to see all of this with them. She closed her eyes as they filled with tears, thinking he was gone forever. But seconds later her eyes sprung open in surprise. She must be imagining things...but she still heard it...*yes!* It was her husband's *voice!* And he was singing their favourite song! She scrambled around, looking in all directions to see him – but all she could see was never-ending stars and space. She stared at Granny and said "I know this sounds daft, but I can hear my Johnny singing our song 'Red, Red, Rose...*up here!*" For a few seconds Granny just stared at Mum, her mouth open in shock at what she'd said, before she replied "My goodness! I never said a word to you in case you thought that I was going a bit daft! I can't hear your husband, but I can hear *my* husband - your Father singing! Can't you *hear* it?" Mum shook her head, saying "No, just my Johnny, singing our song!" she said, smiling as she looked around her. But Granny replied "Well, wherever they are, your Johnny's certainly being more romantic with his singing than your Dad, who I think is being a wee bit cheeky! He's singing 'Shine on Harvest Moon', can you believe it?" They both looked at each other and burst into laughter. Shannon had heard it all and smiled to herself knowing that the singing was *very* real indeed. As soon as Mum had said that she'd heard Daddy singing a silvery web appeared stretching out in front of the bike and straight towards a single star – Shannon knew that this was exactly where they had to go.

Mum and Granny laughed and sang most of the way to the star. The bike slowed down and turned to glide in next to it and gently came to a stop. So did the singing. Shannon lifted her goggles and turned around. Mum and Granny were no longer laughing. They just stared in wonder at this star, which was right *next* to them. Shannon helped them down carefully from the trailer, assuring them that the silvery webs were safe to stand on. They looked all around, their mouths open in amazement. What a wonderful, glowing star. What wonderful, twinkling space all around them, that went on forever. And the Earth down there, now glowing a bluey-green at one side. It was simply….beautiful! "Well" smiled Shannon. "..we're here!" Mum and Granny just nodded, they were still trying to take in this incredible scenery. Shannon said gently "I hope that this cheered you both up at least a little bit." Mum took her hand and looked her in the eyes, whispering "Yes, Shannon. You've done really well, it's *incredible*! But we only wish that your Daddy and Grandad could be up here to see you here with us." They stared sadly back down at the Earth, but Shannon asked "I know that you miss them, but do you *believe* that you'll see them again?" Mum and Granny stayed quiet for a while, until Granny answered "Well, we *should* do Shannon. We hear about life going on whenever we go to church. But it's so hard to believe right now." Shannon thought for a while, before saying "But what do you think

Grandad and Daddy would *like* you to believe?" Mum answered "I suppose that they'd want us to believe that they're alright"

Shannon looked at them and answered "All right Mum....Granny....could you do me a favour and close your eyes please?" They wouldn't normally do that for Shannon, unless it was for a game. But tonight, up here, they felt different. Shannon went on "Now think of a time when you and Grandad or Daddy were so happy!" They both stood with their backs to the star, eyes closed and starting to smile. Shannon continued "Now imagine them asking you to believe that they're with you right now!" Granny and Mum imagined this as they both nodded their heads as their smiles grew even wider. And at that moment they both heard their husbands singing again. Shannon whispered "Now....open your eyes please!" they did. The still heard the singing and saw the Earth glowing far away in front of them and the sun peeking around its edge. Shannon remembered what Grandad had said to her before and asked them "Why do you both keep looking towards the Earth when we talk about Grandad or Daddy? They're not down there at all. They're *always* with you, just like they always promised. In fact they're here with you now!" She smiled, looking over their shoulders into the intense light of the star. At that moment Mum and Granny realised that the sound of Grandad and Daddy's singing wasn't just in their heads – it was coming from the star *behind* them! They both felt a hand gently touching their shoulders. They stopped looking down at the Earth and slowly turned around to face the star as the singing stopped. Their eyes opened wide as they began to make out the shape of two figures in that wonderful, warm glow. Two hands came out and held theirs, gently pulling them in. Mum couldn't speak. She looked at Shannon, as if to ask if it was safe to go into the star. Shannon nodded and said "Mum, Granny, go ahead...it's all right, I promise!" With that they both stepped into the wonderful light and

Shannon stood and watched them slowly disappear into it. A huge grin grew on her face asheard Mum and Granny gasping and crying with such deep happiness inside that light! She followed them into that glowing warmth and saw Mum and Granny hugging Daddy and Grandad, surrounded by that brilliant, golden glow. She had never seen them so happy before, or hug so tightly. Grandad lifted an arm to wave Shannon over to them. She stepped over and they all clung together in a huddle of joy, tears and *belief!* They were closer than ever before – and for the first time, there was no doubt at all that they would be together forever - no matter what!

Chapter 23 - Knowing

Mum and Granny just stood in that sea of wonderful light, staring with happiness at their husband's faces. They didn't know how long they hugged for. No words were needed. All that Mum and Granny knew was that their beloved husbands were not gone – and that was all that was important to them. The first words were gently spoken by Grandad, as he and Daddy started to walk further into the light. "Come on, follow us!" he smiled. "There's a special place that we want you to see." Shannon had never walked far back into a star before. She held Mum and Granny's hands as they all slowly walked forward. The light quickly got too bright to see anything at all, but suddenly they found that they had walked out of the light and into the most amazing and beautiful land that could *possibly* be imagined!

Everything and everywhere were the most *amazing* colours - simply like no colour that had ever been seen on Earth. Under their feet was the thickest, softest, greenest grass anyone could imagine. The most *beautiful* flowers rocked in a soft breeze. A lovely tree stood just in front of them, which seemed to gently dance as its sweetest blossoms of tiny flowers fluttered. They stood amazed at everything they saw. They looked above at a perfect sky. In the distance was a sparkling lake, with towering mountains behind. In the lake was a castle on a small island, with a large, wooden sailing ship beside it. Shannon recognised the castle and ship straight away. Down in front of them by the shore were Grandad and Daddy waving for them to come down and join them. They waved back and Granny suddenly found that she was full of the most incredible energy and started to run down the hill, just like she could as a young girl! Mum laughed and raced after her through the thick grass, rainbow-coloured butterflies fluttering around them. Shannon stood by the tree and laughed as she watched them racing down the hill, but then felt something touching her arm. She looked to her side and there she was "*Reulach*!" she smiled. Uncle Leo's wonderful horse was standing right next to her! Reulach lowered her head as if to ask Shannon to climb on. She leapt on and they galloped down through the grass, before Reulach took off into that *wonderful* sky! Mum and Granny waved up at Shannon as they flew over them! They swooped right over the castle in the lake, before turning and coming in to land on the soft, white sand beside Grandad and Daddy at the lakeside. Shannon clambered off Reulach as Mum and Granny arrived at the bottom of the hill, laughing like small girls - *what* a place! They kept laughing as they sat down on the beach together, which had the most beautiful, white, soft sand.

Shannon looked over at the boat by the castle on the island and said to Grandad "That boat out there, it's our ancestor's galley isn't it Grandad? *You* know, the one in the painting above Uncle Leo's fire? And in the window and picture in the church?" Grandad nodded and replied "Yes, Shannon, that's the one." At that very moment the galley's many rows of long oars lifted up from the water and the empty boat started to row its way across to them all by itself, as if it had heard Shannon talking about it! Shannon gasped! It reminded her a bit of the pictures of Viking long-ships in her schoolbooks. It slowly glided across the clear water towards them. Grandad and Daddy saw it coming and stood up on the soft sand.

Daddy looked down at Shannon and gently said "It's time for Grandad and me to go now." Mum and Granny looked disappointed and Daddy could see that. "But you know now that we're all right and that we're *always* with you; that we all *go on* living, no matter *how* hard that may seem to believe down on Earth. We'll be waiting here for you, so always know that and *don't* be scared." The boat gently touched onto the shore beside them. Shannon looked at it and then said to Grandad "If you and Daddy are going across to the castle in the galley, can we all come with you too?" Grandad smiled, saying "I'm afraid that we can't *choose* when it's anyones time to go, Shannon. Until you've all finished doing what you have to do on Earth the galley won't take you across to the castle. It knows that it's not your time yet. And across in that castle are many people who would *love* to meet you all right now – but as I say, it's not your time yet." He looked around at Mum and Granny and said "But *trust* me when I say that when your life finishes down on Earth that you'll be able to come through the stars yourself. And then the galley will come across the lake here for you and take you to the castle too. And your Daddy, me and your ancestors will have a *fantastic* welcome party for you all in there, I *promise!*"

They wrapped their arms around each other again tightly. As Grandad hugged Shannon he reminded her to keep caring for the stars. Then Daddy and Grandad stepped onto the galley. The oars gently took them across the calm water towards the castle, as they waved, staring back to the shore. Mum smiled as she waved back and whispered "Goodbye!" Granny looked at her and said "I think you meant to say *'See you later'*!" They watched as Grandad and Daddy climbed off the galley onto the small island and then walk up the steps of the castle and open the door, before looking back towards them and happily waving. Mum, Granny and Shannon waved back to them as Granny whispered "See you later Jimmy!"

Mum smiled and said towards the castle "Yes, see you later!" as the door of the castle closed.

As Granny, Mum and Shannon got to the top of the hill by the tree, they took a last look back, for now. Along the top walls of the castle were Grandad, Daddy and many other people, smiling and happily waving to them. As they stood there without saying a word, they all knew that these people were their ancestors. Shannon patted Reulach and left him happily by the tree to graze on the lush green grass and to happily gallop around, until they would see him again.

Their lives were changed forever. Now they had no reason to be afraid of anything and to look forward to absolutely everything! They felt so lucky to have had the chance to see and know, rather than just hope.

Shannon took them to the moon on the way home and they had a wonderful party at Uncle Leo's. He was so happy to see them, even if Granny *did* beat him at golf! Soon they were zooming away from Uncle Leo's on the bike, the Earth was glowing a swirly green and blue below them. But as they got closer they knew that the Earth would never be the same again to them. Now it was *so* much better. Of course there would still be problems down there, but now they knew that *no* problem would really matter in the end, as they'd end up in that *wonderful* land through the stars anyway. They would just happily enjoy life down there and try to help others enjoy their temporary lives down on Earth too! And one day it would be *their* time to leave the Earth for the stars, just like Grandad and Daddy. Simple!

They put the bike away in the museum shed again and walked back through the dark, snowy streets to Mum's house. Granny and Mum spent most of the walk home just staring up at the stars, no longer wondering what they were, but knowing just *how* important they are to us all. Shannon thought that they were going to have awfully sore necks in the morning! When they got home they sat for hours chatting and giggling over cups of cocoa about what had happened that night. They knew not to tell *anyone* about what they had seen. After all, *who* would believe such a story?

Shannon's first day back at school after the New Year was one that she would never forget. As she walked through the school gates she was met by her best pal Louisa, who was so happy to see her and immediately they were giggling and playing together. Although Shannon could never tell her what she'd seen and done, she was so happy for Louisa too, knowing that after this life that they'd have such fun together playing up in that wonderful place! In fact, Shannon looked at everyone happily afterwards, knowing this. They walked in through the school door and into the girl's cloakrooms, only to find Veronica surrounded by her friends from her year. Veronica looked upset, like she'd been crying and it looked like her 'friends' were laughing at *her*! As Shannon hung up her bag Veronica saw her and shouted "There she is, *ask* her!" as she rushed across to Shannon and grabbed her arm. This made her 'friends' laugh at her even more. Shannon waited for Veronica to shout at her, maybe even *hit* her again. But instead Veronica said "*Tell* them Shannon. I saw you flying off from Bunker's Brae on your Grandad's bike on Christmas Day! *Tell* them!" she demanded. Shannon saw the look of panic on her face as the cloakroom filled with laughter around them. Now Veronica was getting some of *her own* medicine! Shannon looked across at Louisa and then back to Veronica and said "Flying? On my Grandad's wobbly old bike? Emmm...I don't *think* so!" The laughter got even louder and Veronica's eyes stared with anger at Shannon and she raised her hand to hit her! But Shannon was saved, as a booming shout of "Girls! Keep the noise down in here and get to your classes!" made the room silent. The room went silent and Mr Morran stood there at his door. Veronica went to storm out of the room past him, but he stopped her, whispering "Veronica Cumberland. I believe that you've been in trouble for knocking over Shannon McNeil before? I'd *hate* to think that you've been nasty to her again. If I *ever* hear that you have been bullying anyone again, you'll be in *serious* trouble, do you *understand*?" Veronica just mumbled "Yes, Mr Morran" and shuffled out the door, her head down in shame.

Veronica never did bother Shannon or Louisa ever again. In fact, she stopped bullying altogether. She got laughed at for a while for trying to tell people about Shannon's flying bike, but that was a good thing! It made her realise that sometimes it's best to keep quiet and that it's never a good thing to laugh at or bully someone for what they do or don't have or what they choose to believe in. Even Veronica's friend Elizabeth never bothered them again! Maybe with Veronica not being a bully any more, there was no point in doing it alone.

Now, we often hear of people "living happily ever after". That generally means that they ended up living in a fancy castle with lots of money. But that's *nothing* compared to what happened to Shannon, Mum and Granny for the rest of their lives here. They had something *far* better. They knew that we go on forever, beyond hope and *even* far more than belief.... they actually *knew*! Now if that's not living 'happily *ever* after', I don't know *what* is!

A few years later Granny and Mum's time was up on Earth. The angels took them back up through the stars to live in that wonderful land with Grandad, Daddy and their ancestors and friends. They even got a chance to meet William, the man who was the first to fly off Bunker's Brae - and *what* laughs they had together!

Shannon happily kept caring for the stars, until it was her turn to pass the job onto another lucky person.

Sometimes every one of us feels afraid, scared or lonely. At times like these we should just look up at the stars. No matter what anybody says, what you do or don't have or how bad things may look, they'll always be up there for you, twinkling, waiting happily and reminding us of how we all go on forever – even if we can't see them for a while until the clouds clear. To hope this is a good thing, to believe it is fantastic. But to know it….is absolutely *amazing*!

The Beginning….!